Miracle on
34th Street

Miracle on 34th Street

Valentine Davies

sandpiper

Houghton Mifflin Harcourt
Boston   New York

Historical Note written by Anna Marlis Burgard

www.hmhbooks.com

The Library of Congress has cataloged an earlier edition as follows:
Davies, Valentine, 1905–1961. Miracle on 34th Street /
Valentine Davies.—1st Harcourt facsimilie edition.
p. cm.
Summary: The lives of three people are changed by
an old man who insists that he is Santa Claus.
1. Santa Claus—Juvenile fiction. [1. Santa Claus—Fiction.
2. Christmas—Fiction. 3. New York (N.Y.)—Fiction.]
I. Title: Miracle on Thirty-fourth Street. II. Title.
PZ7.D2848Mi 2001
[Fic]—dc21   2001001953

ISBN: 978-0-15-216377-8 hardcover
ISBN: 978-0-547-41442-3 paperback

Manufactured in the United States of America
DOM 10 9 8 7 6 5 4 3 2 1
4500245796

For Liz

Author's Note

LIKE everything else about Mr. Kringle, his appearance in book form does not follow any accepted pattern. Instead of appearing first on the printed page and then making his bow upon the screen, Mr. Kringle completely reversed the procedure. His singular personality and the chain reaction which it started originally took shape in my mind as a motion picture story. It was only after he had come to life upon the screen that he was invited to appear within the covers of a book.

I can, therefore, hardly take sole credit for this story in its present form. For George Seaton put Kris into a screenplay for Twentieth Century-Fox and then, as director, brought him to life before the camera. So many of his ideas have been incorporated into this book that it amounts to a collaboration; a collaboration which I gratefully acknowledge.

In behalf of Mr. Kringle I wish to say a very hearty thank you to William Perlberg for believing in him and for producing the picture "Miracle on 34th Street"; and to Twentieth Century-Fox for their generosity in allowing him to appear in book form; and finally to Dr. Walter M. Simpson, who introduced Mr. Kringle to his publishers.

VALENTINE DAVIES

❦ ❦ ❦ I ❦ ❦ ❦

IF you searched every old folks' home in the country, you couldn't find anyone who looked more like Santa Claus. He was the living, breathing incarnation of the old gent—white beard, pink cheeks, fat tummy and all—and his name was Kris Kringle, too. Whether this was coincidence or design—a sort of stage name he had assumed—his friends at the Maplewood Home for the Aged never knew. Nor did they know exactly how old he was. His white whiskers made him look a good seventy-five, and yet when he laughed or walked you would swear he wasn't a day over fifty. His eyes were quick and happy, and he had a smile to match. Not only did Kris look precisely like Santa Claus, he firmly believed he *was* that jolly old gentleman.

Dr. Pierce, the physician at Maplewood, found this delusion innocent and harmless. In fact, the old man's kindly shrewdness in all other respects had

3

won the doctor completely. He was devoted to Kris and was his staunchest defender. He often came to visit his little room at Maplewood. It was littered with toys of all sizes and shapes, half-finished models, and catalogues. Kris spent most of his time there, smoking his pipe and whittling at his toys.

One November morning when Dr. Pierce dropped in, Kris hardly noticed him. He was reading a newspaper advertisement, and his eyes snapped with indignation as he read. A shopping service offered to make all purchases of Christmas gifts well in advance of the holiday and save the subscriber 10% in the bargain. "All you have to do is send us the names and ages of all the people you wish to remember," Kris read aloud. "We will relieve you of the irksome necessity of Christmas shopping." Angrily, Kris threw the paper on the floor.

"Is this what Christmas has degenerated into, Doctor?" he asked. "It's pure commercialism! Is there no true Christmas spirit left in the world?"

Dr. Pierce was afraid not. Christmas had certainly been commercialized. It had become "big business," and the spirit behind it seemed to be lost in the milling crowds that packed all the stores.

Kris was not prepared to believe that, in spite of outward appearances and ads like this. "No, Doctor," he said. "Underneath all the hurry and bustle people still believe in Santa Claus and all Christmas stands for." He suddenly smiled at the Doctor and asked him what *he* wanted for Christmas.

"I'll tell you what I want," said Pierce half to himself. "An X-ray machine. We've needed one here for years."

"You shall have it," Kris said.

The Doctor smiled. "If I get an X-ray machine, I'll *know* you're Santa Claus."

"You just wait, Doctor—you'll see."

Kris picked up a toy and started to whittle away on it, cheerfully pulling at his pipe. But Dr. Pierce was worried. A frown settled over his pleasant face as he watched Kris working. There was something on his mind and he groped for the right words. Finally he forced himself to come right out with it. "Kris, you'll have to leave Maplewood."

"Why?" asked Kris in astonishment.

Well, the Doctor explained, he had been fighting the Board on this for years, but they had finally overruled him and issued a definite order. In fact, there was nothing more Pierce could do.

Kringle still didn't understand.

"Well, Kris, the laws of the State and Maplewood's charter only allow us to keep old people so long as they are in good physical *and* mental health."

"What's the matter with me?" asked Kris.

5

"You've told me I'm in better physical shape than 90 per cent of your patients. And mentally, well, I've passed all your tests with flying colors. Look, I still remember that last one."

Kris proceeded to go through the routine of a simple mental test; adding and subtracting, giving synonyms for words, and so forth. There was no doubt about it, he knew all the answers. Mr. Kringle, in spite of his age, was keen, alert, and exceptionally skillful.

"I know," said the Doctor quietly, "but it's this Kris Kringle business. You know—we've discussed it before."

"You mean because I'm Santa Claus?"

The Doctor nodded slowly.

"But there's nothing wrong about that," said Kris. "It happens to be the truth."

"It's not quite that simple," Pierce replied. "Unfortunately, the Board does not believe in Santa Claus, Kris. So technically you're, well, not acceptable."

"So I'm not sane because the Board of Directors doesn't believe in Santa Claus!"

"That's one way of putting it," admitted Dr. Pierce.

Kris paused and reflected for a moment. "What happens next?" he asked.

Pierce explained that Maplewood had an arrangement with the Mount Hope Sanatorium.

"That nut house?" Kris exploded. "Never!"

"But what's your alternative?" Pierce asked him. "Have you got any money?"

Kris examined a small check book which lay on his desk. He had $34.86.

"Kris, you're pretty old," said Dr. Pierce. "It won't be easy to earn a living. And if you're unsuccessful, you will become a ward of the State. And if you're picked up because you tell somebody you're Santa Claus, you'll be sent to Mount Hope anyway, so why not go direct?"

But Kris was adamant. There was nothing wrong with him and he'd be damned if he was going to an asylum. Dr. Pierce finally conceded that it was really up to Kris. If he left Maplewood, nobody would bother him. That would end the case as far as they were concerned. But what could Kris do? How could he fend for himself? He didn't have much money—where would he stay?

"The zoo keeper in Central Park is a friend of mine. I'll stay with him," Kris answered.

Dr. Pierce urged him to reconsider and accept the transfer philosophically. "You'll have time to think it over. We'll talk about it again," he said as he moved toward the door.

7

Kris nodded silently, but there was a look of determination on the old man's face. The moment the Doctor had gone, he hauled out a large suitcase from his closet and briskly began to pack.

♣ ♣ ♣ **2** ♣ ♣ ♣

THE Central Park Zoo was nearly deserted at this early hour. In one of the enclosures a keeper was tidying up in anticipation of a busy day. As the white-bearded figure approached, the keeper greeted him eagerly with a wave of his shovel.

"How are you, Kris?" he called.

"Fine, Jim! Never better," said the old man heartily. "And how are the boys?"

"Gettin' fat and lazy," Jim told him, smiling, "and it's mostly your fault!"

Kris laughed and gave a whistle. From within the shed a reindeer's head peered shyly out, then another. The old man called again and held out a handful of carrots. In a few minutes half a dozen reindeer were eating out of his hand.

Jim stood silently by and watched this performance, smiling. Kris sure had an uncanny way with animals! Jim had fed and fussed over these critters

9

for a dozen years and he couldn't get near them. But even the timid does would eat right out of Kris' hand. Jim had never ceased to be amazed at this. It was a bond between him and Kris.

"Jim, I may need a place to stay. Could you put me up for a while?" asked Kris.

"Why, certainly, Kris, as long as you want. There's plenty of room," Jim assured him.

Fully satisfied that all was well, Kris started on his way again, swinging along with his exuberant, youthful gait. He had no special destination, but he loved being outdoors in this crisp cold air. If only there were snow on the ground, he thought, this would be a perfect day. As the old gentleman approached the western limits of the park, he suddenly stopped and cocked his head to one side, listening. His keen ears had picked up an exciting sound. It was faint but unmistakable. Somewhere in the distance a band was playing *Jingle Bells*. It seemed to be coming from just outside the park. Kris turned and made for the nearest exit.

Central Park West and especially the side streets leading into it were filled with color and confusion as Kris arrived upon the scene. For the Macy Parade was about to start amid indescribable excitement. Sponsored annually by the R. H. Macy Department Store, it was every child's dream of a Christmas Parade, or as near as mere adults could make it. A sharp wind was blowing the huge inflated figures every which way. A Pilgrim Father; Jack the Giant Killer; a Panda; and an enormous ice cream cone careened crazily about, towering two or three stories into the air. The costumed men who held the guide ropes seemed like frantic Lilliputians. Sleepy, Grumpy, Dopey, and the other dwarfs, scampered about and climbed aboard their floats. So did a myriad of other famous characters. A dozen bands in fancy uniforms were loudly tuning up.

The person who seemed to be in charge of the whole business was a handsome, well-dressed, businesslike young woman. She was checking off various people on a list. Kris heard them address her as "Mrs. Walker." Assisting her was a spectacled, bald-headed and very much harried gentleman named Mr. Shellhammer.

The thing which really fascinated Kris was the last float in the Parade—Santa Claus in his sleigh, pulled by eight wooden but very realistic reindeer. The Santa Claus was practicing with his whip in a wild and lurching manner as Kris sauntered up. Kris stood watching as long as he could. Then he stepped up and with a polite "Allow me, sir," took the whip from his hand. With a single expert flip of the wrist he flicked the long whip. The end crackled smartly one inch over the farthest reindeer's ear.

"You see, it's all in the wrist," he said. But Macy's Santa wasn't impressed. One whiff of his breath told Kris the reason. The man grabbed for a pint bottle, not too well hidden beneath his blanket, taking more and more frequent nips.

Kris was shocked and horrified. The idea of a drunk depicting Santa Claus to thousands of impressionable children infuriated him. He started toward Mrs. Walker to register an outraged protest. But the young lady was suddenly standing next to him, beckoning for the float to move ahead. Before Kris could speak, it suddenly lurched forward and the saturated Santa nearly toppled off the float.

It didn't take Mrs. Walker long to size up the situation. This man was really drunk and she was responsible for all personnel. She fired him on the spot.

"Just think if Mr. Macy had seen him," said Mr. Shellhammer in a horrified tone.

"Just think if Mr. *Gimbel* had seen him!" said Mrs. Walker in even greater horror.

Now the whole parade was ready to start, and they had no Santa Claus. Mrs. Walker and Shellhammer saw Kris at the same time. They pounced upon him together.

"Would you be Santa Claus?" she asked him.

"Have you had any experience?" Mr. Shellhammer inquired. This last question struck the old man's funnybone. His little round body shook with inward chuckles.

"Yes," he said. "A little."

"Then you've got to help us out. Please!"

"Madam," Kris replied with quiet dignity, "I am not in the habit of substituting for spurious Santa Clauses."

Mrs. Walker pleaded and coaxed, but the old man was firm. Not even money seemed to interest him.

"Well, we can't hold the Parade up any longer," said Mr. Shellhammer. "We'll have to go on without a Santa Claus."

Kris looked off toward the crowd of excited children lining the streets. And then he realized that he had no alternative. He couldn't disappoint those eager faces.

"All right," he said, handing his hat and cane to Shellhammer. "Get me the clothes. I'll do it!"

A few minutes later, Kris found himself the leading figure of this great Parade moving down the long avenue, waving and smiling at thousands of children, cracking his whip and having the time of his life.

13

❦ ❦ ❦ 3 ❦ ❦ ❦

WHEN she had finally managed to get the Parade under way, Doris Walker, exhausted and frozen, returned to her apartment on Central Park West. The Parade was passing right by the building, but Doris pushed through the crowd and entered without giving it so much as a glance. She didn't care if she never saw a parade again. All she wanted was a hot bath.

Doris opened the door to her small and sternly modern apartment and called "Susan—Susan!" There was no reply. But Cleo, the maid, poked her head out of the kitchen and said that Susan was in "Uncle" Fred's apartment watching the Parade. Doris walked to the living-room window and looked out. From her inside apartment, the only view was directly into the rear windows of the front apartment across the court. Doris rapped loudly on the glass and in a moment Fred appeared at the opposite window. They waved a greeting and Doris shouted that she'd be over in a little while.

"Uncle" Fred was no relation of Susan's at all. Young and attractive, Fred Gayley was a lawyer with one of the city's oldest law firms. Being neighbors, he and Susan had become great pals and out of this had grown a pleasant and casual friendship between Fred and Doris. It was far more casual than Fred would have liked. But Doris' first marriage had ended in divorce and from her grim avoidance of any reference to it, Fred gathered that it had been a bitter disillusionment. At any rate she seemed determined to avoid further entanglement. She was pleasant and friendly enough to Fred but the real Doris would never emerge from her shell —even for a fleeting minute.

Fred's apartment faced Central Park West and from its windows he and Susan, a rather serious child of six, had a perfect view of the gay and colorful Parade. The sound of band music and cheering children filled the air. But, as usual, Fred was filled with much more childlike wonder and excitement than his little companion. As one of the huge, inflated figures passed the window, Fred said eagerly:

"That's Jack the Giant Killer, isn't it? And look! The great big fellow is the giant!"

15

"Of course," said little Susan, "there are no giants, really."

"Maybe not now, Susan—but in the olden days . . ."

Susan shook her head firmly.

"People sometimes grow very tall—but that is abnormal. Mommy told me."

Fred studied the child for a moment as she unexcitedly watched the Parade. He couldn't help but feel sorry for her. True, she was intelligent—maybe too much so for a child of her age—but there was no gaiety about her. Fun was a stranger to Susan.

"Maybe your Mother's right," said Fred meekly, "but I believe in giants anyhow!"

When Doris arrived, she launched into a caustic and detailed account of all her troubles with the soused Santa. Fred tried to quiet her with gestures and grimaces. But it was no use. Finally, using a cup of coffee as a pretext, he dragged Doris into his tiny kitchenette and begged her not to expose all these disillusioning facts to her daughter.

But Doris had very definite ideas about bringing up children. She believed in utter realism and truth. Susan was certainly *not* going to be led to believe a lot of myths and legends—like Santa Claus, for example.

"Why not?" asked Fred. "What harm does it do?"

"They grow up considering life as a big fairy tale instead of reality," Doris answered. "Subconsciously they keep waiting for Prince Charming to come along and when he does and turns out to be—"

"Look, Doris," Fred's voice was kindly, "you had a tough break—I'm not denying that. You loved someone deeply—you trusted him—and then one day you suddenly woke up and found how wrong you'd been. But all men aren't like that and I don't think Susan's going to be any happier growing up to think so."

Doris turned away. Fred's directness had found its target.

"I'm sorry," he went on, "but I'm right, Doris." He moved closer to her. "And I only wish you'd give me a chance to prove that I'm really the sort of person that—well, you hoped he was."

"I've burnt my fingers once," Doris answered quietly.

She turned back toward the living room and Fred, with a hopeless shrug, followed.

❦ ❦ ❦ 4 ❦ ❦ ❦

EARLY the next morning, looking very smart and businesslike, Mrs. Walker entered her office at Macy's. There sat Kris waiting patiently to see her. Doris was the Personnel Director of the store and Mr. Shellhammer, Head of the Toy Department, had suggested that Kris be given a permanent job as Macy's Santa Claus. For Kris had made a tremendous hit at the Parade and the ceremonies which followed. He was by far the most authentic Santa Claus that they had ever found. Mr. Shellhammer was most enthusiastic. This man was incredibly convincing; he would boom the Toy Department's sales immeasurably.

Kris told Doris that he would be very happy to accept the job. Doris hired him instantly, grateful for having one headache less this year, for the Santa Claus had always been a problem. The salary and other details did not seem to interest Kris. Doris buzzed for her assistant, Miss Adams, who took him to her office and asked him to fill out an employment card. Kris sat down and filled out the form in a clear, Spencerian hand:

NAME: Kris Kringle
ADDRESS: Maplewood Home, Great Neck, Long Island
AGE: As old as my tongue and a little bit older than my teeth.

He handed the card to Miss Adams. She glanced at it mechanically as she turned and started for Mrs. Walker's office. "Thank you, Mr. Kringle. Mr. Shellhammer's waiting for you."

Mr. Shellhammer took Kris to the locker room to change into his Santa Claus outfit. While he dressed, Shellhammer handed Kris a list of the stock of the Toy Department. He had checked the particular items which were to be pushed this year. Kris nodded understandingly and from the few remarks he made he seemed to have an amazing knowledge of Macy's toys. Mr. Shellhammer emphasized the fact that if a child asked for something they did not carry, Kris was to suggest an item which they wanted to push. Mr. Kringle nodded silently—almost grimly. He knew exactly what Mr. Shellhammer meant. As soon as he left, Kris tore the list into very small pieces.

✦

Enthroned on the dais, with a long line of eager kiddies waiting to see him Kris was really in his element. He loved every minute of it and so did all the boys and girls. There were many remarks among parents about how very real this Santa Claus seemed. Everything was perfect. Mr. Shellhammer looked out of his office and beamed happily.

"And what do you want for Christmas?" Kris asked, as a little boy climbed up on his ample lap.

"I want a fire engine," the youngster replied, "the kind that's got real hoses that squirt real water, and I promise not to squirt it in the house only outside in the yard."

Behind the boy's back his mother was frantically gesturing for Kris not to promise delivery on the fire wagon, but Kris paid no attention.

"All right, sonny," he said, "I'm sure you're a good boy—you'll get one."

Delighted, the child climbed down. Now it was the mother's turn to say a word or two. She was fuming but spoke quietly so the boy could not hear.

"Why did you tell him that? They're not making that kind of fire engines. I've looked everywhere."

"Oh, but you *can* get them," Kris replied, "at the Acme Toy Company at 246 West 26th Street. They're eight-fifty—a wonderful bargain."

The woman stared in amazement. She couldn't

believe her ears. Was Macy's Santa Claus sending her to another store? Kris replied that he certainly was, and he couldn't see anything particularly strange about it. After all, the important thing was to make the kiddies happy and whether Macy's or Acme sold the toy didn't make any great difference.

And so Kris continued as child after child climbed upon his lap. His only thought was for the youngsters —he wanted to be sure each boy and girl would get his wish at Christmas. If the toys seemed too expensive, or Macy's didn't carry them, Kris told the mother just where she could get a less expensive train for Johnny, or where she would find just the doll for Judy. The parents were inevitably both surprised and pleased.

It was unfortunate, therefore, that Mr. Shellhammer should have overheard Mr. Kringle advising a little boy's mother to go to Gimbel's for his skates. Gimbel's, of all places! Mr. Shellhammer went into a mild state of shock. As soon as he regained his self-control he started for Mrs. Walker's office. He was determined to have Kringle fired right away. This was simply inconceivable! If word of it ever got back to Mr. Macy—the Lord only knew what would happen!

But as he proceeded through the store he was stopped by a number of grateful mothers. They couldn't thank him enough for this tremendously helpful service. Instead of being merely commercial, Macy's Santa was actually being helpful to parents! It was a wonderful thing. The real Christmas spirit. They would never forget it. They would be regular Macy customers from now on. Mr. Shellhammer began to wonder. He stopped off at his own office and there were many grateful messages and notes. Mr. Shellhammer sat down at his desk to think things over. Perhaps his first reaction had been wrong.

"I think it's a wonderful idea!" his secretary told him as she delivered another batch of notes.

"You think so, and the women think so," he said sadly, "but will *Mr. Macy* think so?"

He looked beseechingly toward the ceiling, but the answer was not there.

❦ ❦ ❦ 5 ❦ ❦ ❦

FRED had a date to take little Susan out that afternoon. And still disturbed by her precociousness, he was hatching out a deep-dyed plot. He would take Susan to see the new Santa Claus at Macy's. That gentleman would worm out of her a Christmas wish, and Fred would arrange to have it under the tree. Perhaps then Susan might believe in Santa Claus, or at least begin to have some normal child-like wonder.

Fred managed to get to Kris and enlist his aid, but when Susan reached the head of the line and Mr. Kringle took her upon his lap, she refused to ask for anything. Whatever she wanted her mother would get her, provided, of course, it wasn't too expensive. She told Kris he was merely the gentle-man her mother had employed this year to play the part of Santa Claus.

"You *are* a little better than most," said Susan. "Anyway, your beard looks real."

Mr. Kringle answered that it was real, and that *he* was real, too. But he could get nowhere with the child. Kris was baffled and troubled. This was just the sort of thing he feared was happening in the world.

As luck would have it, Doris emerged from her office just as this was going on and started walking briskly toward the elevator. She glanced toward the dais—and then stopped dead. There was her daughter on Santa Claus' lap. Fred saw her approaching and looked a little sheepish. There was no scene at all. Doris was brusque and definite. She quickly whisked Susan away from Kris and planted her in a chair near the office. Then she asked Fred to step inside.

From her vantage point Susan watched Kris as he took a little girl with golden pigtails upon his lap. Her foster mother was explaining to Kris that the child had only recently arrived from an orphanage in Holland. She spoke hardly a word of English; but the wide-eyed child had insisted that "Sinterklaas," as she called him, should speak Dutch. The girl was confidently talking away to Kris and her mother's anguish was obvious. She started to explain to the girl, but Kris raised his hand for silence, and when

24

the child had finished he answered her in fluent Dutch. The sudden light which warmed the little Dutch girl's eyes did a funny thing to Susan. She stood there fascinated as Kris and the girl happily sang a little Dutch Christmas song together. There was something very real about this Santa Claus and it puzzled her considerably.

Inside her office, Doris had minced no words with Fred. She appreciated his interest and kindness toward her daughter but Susan was still *her* responsibility—to bring up as she saw fit. Whether Fred agreed with her or not she insisted that he respect her wishes regarding the child. Fred took the scolding he knew he deserved. He promised not to repeat the performance if Doris would let him go on being friends with Susan. Very contritely he said goodnight to Susan and Doris and departed.

As soon as Susan was alone with her mother, she began asking questions about Mr. Kringle. Doris carefully explained that he was just an employee of the store, like the doorman or the elevator man or anyone else.

"Yes, I know," said Susan, "but when he started speaking Dutch to that little girl, Mother—"

"Susan, I speak French," said Doris patiently, "but that doesn't make me Joan of Arc."

But Susan was not convinced. A shred of doubt

25

still lingered in her mind. This Mr. Kringle had such a twinkle in his eyes.

In order to clear up any confusion in her daughter's mind, Doris sent for Kris immediately. He entered with a jolly wink and smile to Susan.

"You're an employee of this store, aren't you?" she asked him. Kris nodded with mild surprise. "And you're not Santa Claus, of course, because there really is no such person."

"I'm sorry to contradict you, Mrs. Walker," Kris replied. "But there certainly is, and here I stand to prove it!"

Susan's eyes opened wide. Her mother looked quite annoyed.

"No, no, you don't understand," she said. "I want you to be perfectly honest in front of the child."

"I *am* being perfectly honest!" said Kris.

Doris tried another tack.

"What is your name?" she asked him.

"Kris Kringle."

Doris pulled Kris' employment card from the file on her desk and she suddenly stiffened.

"Is there anything more I can tell you?" he was asking.

But Mrs. Walker was really frightened now. "No —no—thank you!" she said hastily as she ushered Susan from the room. This man really believed that he was Santa Claus! This "gem" that she had found might be a dangerous character! He seemed kindly and innocent enough, but who knew what other manifestations he might show! And he had been with countless children all day long! It was a wonder that nothing serious had happened. She had just found out in time.

Quietly but firmly she gave Kris his notice. She wanted no trouble. She arranged to give him two weeks' pay. The old man didn't seem to mind. His only reaction seemed to be concern for Doris and little Susan. It was almost as if Doris were the one whose mental state was to be pitied.

As Mr. Kringle walked out of the door the phone rang. Mr. Macy wished to see her immediately. Doris entered the holy of holies with fear and trepidation. Had Macy found out that she'd hired a nut? And when she saw Mr. Shellhammer there as well, her heart skipped a few more beats.

To her amazement, Mr. Macy congratulated both of them. Already word of Mr. Kringle's recommendations had reached him. Mr. Macy was being flooded with wires, phone calls, and messages of appreciation from grateful parents. This was the biggest goodwill idea that had ever hit the store. Why, it was revolutionary! Macy's Santa recommending Gimbel's! The results were bound to be phenomenal. He intended to make it the policy throughout the store. "The Store with the *Real* Christmas Spirit." It was tremendous—a brand new departure in merchandising policy, and Macy's would reap the harvest of publicity and good will. They must by all means keep this Santa Claus. Perhaps they could even find some other work for him after the holidays. Mr. Macy was delighted. He promised both Doris and Shellhammer immediate raises.

Outside Mr. Macy's office, Doris shakily broke the news to Shellhammer. She had just fired their wonderful Santa; the old man was definitely crazy. Mr. Shellhammer exploded. They must get him back at once—before he left the store. If they didn't, all was lost!

Doris said they could get another Santa Claus to carry out the same policy. But Mr. Macy had brought his grandson to see Kringle that afternoon, Shellhammer told her. He had been tremendously impressed—they must get Kringle back at any cost!

After a frantic search Doris finally caught Kris in the service elevator. She told him that she had reconsidered and that he still could have the job. But to her dismay, Mr. Kringle politely declined. "I'm afraid I don't like your attitude," he said frankly, "nor Mr. Shellhammer's either!" Frantically Doris tried to explain that his genuine helpfulness and kindness had caused a sensation.

"You *must* stay and keep on spreading good will. Why, even Mr. Macy——"

Kris, however, was adamant. Mrs. Walker had clearly indicated her cynical disbelief. That was enough for him.

But when Doris broke down and told him the whole story and explained that if he left it would mean her job, Mr. Kringle's whole attitude changed. If that were the case, he said, he would certainly stay. He couldn't have Mrs. Walker losing her job, not just before the holidays. "Think what that would mean to your lovely little daughter," he said.

For Kris had begun to realize that Doris and little Susan were but unhappy products of their times. They presented a real challenge to him—a sort of test-case for Santa Claus. If he could win them over, if he could get them to believe in him—then there was still hope. If not, Santa Claus and all he stood for were through.

"You know, Mrs. Walker," he said, "for the past fifty years or so I've been more and more worried about Christmas. It seems we're all so busy trying to beat the other fellow in making things go faster and look shinier and cost less, that Christmas and I are sort of getting lost in the shuffle."

"Oh, I don't think so," said Doris. "Christmas is still Christmas."

"No," said Mr. Kringle, shaking his head. "Christmas isn't just a day. It's a frame of mind. That's what's been changing. That's why I'm glad I'm here, because maybe I can do something about it."

In spite of herself, Doris was impressed by Kris' warmth and kindness. She couldn't help liking the old man, even if he was a little off the beam.

✤ ✤ ✤ 6 ✤ ✤ ✤

THE next morning Kris was back on the dais once more—and everybody was happy. The line of children was longer than ever. Kris' reputation had already begun to grow. Word of mouth was spreading the news of the honest and kindly old gentleman at Macy's. But in Doris' mind there lingered a definite doubt and a worry. After all, *she* had employed him and although he seemed harmless enough, she knew very little about the old man. He certainly had this delusion and he might not be as harmless as he seemed. At any rate, she had better make sure. She studied his employment card again. Address: Maplewood Home, Great Neck, Long Island, it said. Just out of curiosity Doris looked it up in the telephone book. To her surprise she found that such a home was listed. Considerably encouraged, she called the place.

But the results were hardly helpful. Yes, a Mr.

Kringle had lived there but he was away. Any questions concerning his physical and mental condition would have to be taken up with Dr. Pierce, the Resident Physician, but he, too, was away that day. Doris left a request for Dr. Pierce to call her, and hung up more concerned than ever. Somewhat reluctantly and as a last resort, Doris called in Mr. Sawyer.

Albert Sawyer was Macy's expert on vocational guidance and psychology, a pompous little gentleman who knew absolutely all the answers. Perhaps this sort of thing was not exactly in his field, Doris suggested hesitantly. But Mr. Sawyer assured her he was just the man. Why, he had made quite a study of Abnormal Psychology! He would be happy to interview this fellow and give her his opinion.

So Kris was ushered into Mr. Sawyer's presence and Sawyer proceeded to "examine" him. Mental tests were nothing new to Mr. Kringle. He knew them all by heart. He had passed them with flying colors a dozen times. Mr. Sawyer's questions were just like all the rest. Who was the first President of the United States? How much was three times five? Kris answered them all as patiently as he could. But Sawyer's self-importance rubbed the old gentleman the wrong way, and the nervous, barking manner in which he asked the questions irritated Kris more and more. How was his eyesight? His hearing? Was his memory good? He went on and on. Now Sawyer held up three fingers in front of Kris' nose. "How many fingers do you see?" he asked.

"Three," answered Kris, "and I see that you bite your nails, Mr. Sawyer. You're quite nervous, aren't you? Do you sleep well nights?"

"That's no concern of yours," snapped Sawyer. "How much is three times five?"

"Fifteen," said Kris. "You asked me that before. Nervous habits like yours are often the result of insecurity. Are you happy at home, Mr. Sawyer?"

This was more than Sawyer could stand. Kris had apparently touched a sore point.

"That will be all, Mr. Kringle," he said coldly. "You may go."

"Thank you," said Kris as he rose, "and take it easy, Mr. Sawyer. Get out in the fresh air more. Get some exercise. Relax."

Doris returned from lunch to find Dr. Pierce waiting to see her. She was delighted to see him. There was something reassuring in his easy, quiet manner. He had come to talk about Mr. Kringle. He had seen Kris' picture in the paper and was delighted to learn that the old gentleman had found this job. There were just a few things, however, that Doris ought to know. Kris had some definite peculiarities.

"Yes!" said Doris. "We found that out."

"They're absolutely harmless," Dr. Pierce assured her. "There are thousands of people leading perfectly normal lives who have similar mild delusions. Like that fellow who claims he's a Russian Prince. He's been proven wrong time after time but nothing has ever shaken his story. And look at him, he's a highly respected and successful restaurateur in Hollywood!"

The Doctor had known and loved Kris for a long time. All Doris' fears were absolutely groundless, he assured her. "Mr. Kringle is incapable of harming anyone," he explained. "His delusion is for good. He just wants to be friendly and helpful." The Doctor's only concern was for the old man's welfare. He wanted to be sure that Kris was all right.

"It would be a little better, I think, if someone would keep on eye on him . . . I mean after working hours. You know, Kris is a very old man and I hate to think of him wandering about New York all alone." Doris was grateful and relieved. She promised Dr. Pierce that this would be done.

Mr. Sawyer wore an imposing frown as he entered Mrs. Walker's office with Mr. Shellhammer. "This man has a definite fixed delusion," Sawyer told her. Doris knew that, but the Doctor from the Maplewood Home had just convinced her that he was perfectly sweet and harmless. But Sawyer was not convinced. He could not be sure from one examination. "Cases like this often become violent when their delusion is attacked." Mr. Sawyer had made a special study of them. If this man were kept on here, he could take no responsibility in this matter. Doris said *she* would then. She was certain that Dr. Pierce knew what he was talking about. Sawyer rose to leave. "I warn you, then, Mrs. Walker, that I wash my hands of the whole affair. If this man grows violent—if something happens—the responsibility will be entirely yours!"

In spite of this warning, Doris and Shellhammer agreed that, as far as Mr. Kringle was concerned, their worries were over. All that was necessary was for someone to keep an eye on him—sort of take custody of him.

"I think that's a splendid solution," said Mr. Shellhammer. "And, of course, you're *just* the person to do it, Mrs. Walker!"

"Oh, no!" said Doris, shaking her head. "I live all alone with my daughter. How can I have him stay with me?"

"Well," said Shellhammer, thoughtfully, "my boy's away at school. We *do* have an empty room."

"Wonderful!" said Doris.

"But I'll have to arrange it with Mrs. Shellhammer first, and that will take a little doing. I'll tell you what. If you'll take him home to dinner tonight, I'll talk to my wife and call you up later."

And so it was agreed.

❧ ❧ ❧ 7 ❧ ❧ ❧

IN spite of Dr. Pierce, Doris was just a little bit apprehensive about having Mr. Kringle in her home. The dinner would be quite an ordeal she was afraid. So she called Fred and invited him as a form of insurance. Fred accepted eagerly, especially when he learned who the guest of honor was to be. He even supplied the entree—a fine venison steak which a friend at the office had given him. Cleo had her own special way of preparing it. It looked very tempting, indeed, but Mr. Kringle couldn't touch a mouthful. He was most apologetic.

"It's not that I'm a vegetarian," he explained. "I love steak or pork or mutton, you know. But deer meat—well, I just couldn't"!

As a matter of fact, Kris turned out to be quite a gourmet, expounding on many kinds of choice dishes and how they should be cooked. Apparently he had come by his vast tummy honestly through years of hearty eating. The dinner actually went off far better than Doris had expected.

Fred and Doris helped Cleo with the dishes and Mr. Kringle seized the opportunity to have a little talk with Susan. All through dinner he had been studying her solemn, wistful little face and hoping for just such a chance as this. Susan had been studying the old man, too. She was very puzzled by him. She knew her mother was right, of course. Mr. Kringle couldn't be Santa Claus because that was only another silly myth. And yet Mr. Kringle was different from anyone she had ever seen before. His talk with the little Dutch girl had made a deep impression, and when he had told her mother that he was Santa, it hadn't seemed silly to her at all. She knew it couldn't be true, but she secretly wished that it would be.

"And what sort of games do you play with the other children?" Mr. Kringle wanted to know. Susan didn't play with them very much, she told him. The games they played were silly.

"What sort of games?" Kris asked.

"Well, today they were playing zoo," said Susan scornfully. "All of them were animals. They asked me what kind of an animal I wanted to be. I didn't want to be an animal, so I didn't play."

"Why didn't you tell them you were a lion or a bear?"

"Because I'm *not* a lion. I'm a little girl," said Susan flatly.

"But the other children weren't animals, either. They were just pretending."

"That's what makes the game so silly."

"I don't feel that way at all," said Kris. "It's really a lot of fun, if you know how to play it. But of course you've got to use your imagination. Do you know what the imagination is, Susan?"

The child nodded sagely. "That's when you see things that aren't really there."

"Well, not exactly," said Kris with a smile. "No —to me the imagination is a place all by itself. A very wonderful country. You've heard of the British Nation and the French Nation?"

Susan nodded again.

"Well, this is the Imagination. And once you get there you can do almost anything you want. How would you like to make snowballs in the summertime? Or drive a big bus down Fifth Avenue? How would you like to have a ship of your own that makes daily trips to China and Australia?"

Susan's face broke into a quiet little smile. Perhaps this *was* silly but it was a lot of fun to think about.

"How would you like to be the Statue of Liberty in the morning and fly south with a flock of geese in the afternoon?"

Susan nodded eagerly in spite of herself. "Well, it's very simple really," Kris said. "All it takes is a little practice. Wouldn't you like to try?"

"Yes," said Susan softly.

"I thought so," said Mr. Kringle, beaming. "Now then let's start in with something easy. How would you like to be a monkey in the zoo? That sounds like fun, eh?"

"I'd like to," said Susan, "but I don't know how to be a monkey, Mr. Kringle."

"Sure you do!" said Kris with assurance. "Now just bend over a little—that's right—and curl your hands in."

And so the first lesson began. Susan was a little slow and self-conscious at first, but in a few minutes she began to get the hang of it and much to his delight, Kris found that he had a very apt and eager pupil.

In the kitchen Doris was wishing out loud that Mr. Shellhammer would call and take Mr. Kringle off her hands. She didn't like the idea of Kris' influence over Susan—even for one evening. Fred, on the other hand, was delighted. Kris, he felt, was just what the doctor ordered for a far too serious six-year-old.

"You ought to have him up for dinner often," Fred suggested.

"No, thank you!" said Doris emphatically. "He's a sweet old man but the less he's around Susan, the better I'll like it."

With a hopeless shrug Fred picked up a silver platter.

"Where does this go?" he asked.

"In the living room," said Doris, "on the second shelf."

As Fred came into the room the lesson was at its height. With amazing rapidity Susan had evolved from a monkey to a fairy queen. With a royal touch of her magic wand she was about to render Mr. Kringle, her faithful knight, invisible. Fred watched this performance with astonishment and delight. It was a crying shame, he thought, that Susan could not see more of Mr. Kringle, for in Kris he saw the perfect antidote for Doris' undeviating skepticism. And a little more contact with the old man might do wonders for Doris, herself. If only there were some way. Then suddenly Fred had a brilliant idea.

"Where are you staying, Mr. Kringle?" he asked.

Kris explained that he was temporarily living with his friend, Jim, the zoo keeper. He felt, however, that he was imposing and he would have to find some other place. Fred jumped at the chance. He had an extra bed in his apartment and he would be delighted to have Mr. Kringle stay with him. Kris was quick to accept. It would give him a chance to see more of Susan and her mother, and that was what he wanted more than anything.

In the kitchen, Doris was talking to Mr. Shell-hammer on the phone. He had encountered considerable difficulty with his wife, but he would keep his promise. He would take Mr. Kringle in. Doris put the receiver down for a moment and went into the living room.

"What do you think?" she said to Kris, with an air of great surprise. "Mr. Shellhammer wants to know if you'd like to stay with him! He lives right near the store and it would be so handy for you."

But Mr. Kringle declined with thanks. He had already accepted Mr. Gayley's invitation.

"Mr. Gayley?" asked Doris, dumbfounded. She turned and glanced at Fred. He was nodding and smiling innocently. So Fred had double-crossed her! With a grim "I see," she went back into the kitchen to tell Mr. Shellhammer that Mr. Kringle had made previous arrangements.

And so Kris gathered his few simple belongings and moved in with Fred that night. Just as he was about to turn the light out, Fred looked over at Mr. Kringle, snugly settled in the other bed. "I'm very glad to have you, Mr. Kringle," he confessed, "because now I'll find out something I've always wanted to know. Does Santa sleep with his whiskers in or out of the blankets?"

"Always sleep with 'em out," said Kris. "The cold air makes 'em grow!"

✿ ✿ ✿ 8 ✿ ✿ ✿

TO Doris, Mr. Kringle was still just a slightly
touched old gentleman. But in the next few days
she found that, sane or not, his influence was spreading amazingly and with astonishing results. Mr.
Macy had carried out his plan to put Kris' policy
into effect. Every employee throughout the great
store cheerfully recommended other concerns and
products to his customers. He had followed this up
with a series of large advertisements in all the New
York papers. Not only had Macy's already gained
many new accounts, but the idea was spreading to
other stores.

One block down from 34th Street, for example,
Mr. Gimbel threw the Macy ad angrily across his
desk and turned to his assembled staff.

"Why didn't one of you think of this?" he fumed.
"Now Macy is suddenly a benevolent spirit, thinking
only of the welfare of the public! And what does

that make me? A profiteering money-grubber. Well, two can play at this game! From now on if we haven't got what a customer wants, send him over to Macy's!"

And so it started to grow. Other stores quickly followed suit. This new idea became the subject of editorials in the newspapers. Articles began to appear in magazines. Radio comedians made quips about it. Almost over night it spread from coast to coast. Mr. Kringle, the center and symbol of the whole idea, was receiving an incredible amount of publicity.

In spite of herself, Doris was impressed. She admitted as much as she and Kris went home together one evening. "Little did I dream," she told him, "when I saw you standing next to that float that I was picking out the man who was going to revolutionize the entire merchandising business!"

"Neither did I," Kris admitted.

"I'm very glad that I did it," said Doris. Mr. Kringle smiled happily. It was the first good sign and he was quite encouraged.

He seemed to be making progress in other directions, for on Sunday, Kris went for a walk in the park with his cane on one arm and Susan on the other. Inevitably they wound up at the zoo. Kris stopped to feed the reindeer. As usual, they came running to him and ate out of his hand. Susan was very much impressed. It wasn't just the reindeer, either. Being with Mr. Kringle was always an exciting adventure. He was full of all sorts of jokes and jingles and stories. Her mother would not approve, she felt sure, but it was a lot of fun.

Now, as they walked along together, the old man broached the subject of her Christmas wish. It didn't seem right to him that a little girl like Susan had no wishes at all. She must want something. Every child did. Susan hesitated a long time before she answered. She had only one wish—and it was a big one. If he really was Santa Claus, she thought to herself, he could make it come true. And so she told Kris her one wish was for a house—a *real* house, not a toy one—where she and her mother could live. Living in a New York apartment was not much fun for a girl her age. The house would have a real big yard with trees in it, and a swing, then she could just run out and play any time she wanted, instead of having to wait for Cleo or someone to take her to Central Park. Kris gulped. "That's quite a tall order," he admitted, "but I'll do my best."

"Well," said Susan with conviction, "if you're really Santa you can get it for me! And if you can't, then you're only a nice man with a white beard, like Mother says!"

Kris realized the challenge. Susan was a mighty shrewd little girl and she had placed him squarely on the spot. From inside her little purse she took the very worn and folded page of a magazine and handed it to him. It was a drawing, an architect's dream of a charming little Colonial home. Susan explained the floor plan to Kris in great detail. Whew! What a tough order, thought the old man, as he pocketed the drawing. He began to worry a little himself.

"Every child can't get every wish," Kris told her, "but that doesn't mean that there isn't a Santa Claus. Some children wish for things they couldn't use if they got them. Lots of little boys want real locomotives, for example. Why, they couldn't even get them into their houses. And little girls wish for baby brothers and sisters, even though their parents wouldn't be able to care for them properly. And besides," he continued, "if every child got what he wanted right away, life wouldn't be half so much fun now, would it? Sometimes it's better to keep on wishing, so that when you get your wish you really appreciate it! In other words," Kris concluded, "there are lots of reasons why every wish a child makes can't come true."

Susan could see that he was right in certain cases. "But I've wished for this house a long time, Mr. Kringle," she told him, "and I'll appreciate it if I get it!" There was nothing more that Kris could say. It was up to him now, and he knew it.

That night, as Fred and he were going to bed, Mr. Kringle began his campaign. He realized that there was only one way he could make Susan's wish come true. Mr. and Mrs. Fred Gayley might live in such a house, but Doris Walker could obviously never swing it alone. And so he casually questioned Fred about his relationship with Doris. Fred was very frank about it. He admitted being in love with Doris, but he also admitted that he could make no headway at all. He told Kris the story of her first marriage and what it had done to Doris. Now her whole life was organized about her daughter and her career, to the complete exclusion of any normal social activities. Doris saw to it that she had no private life at all.

Kris nodded sadly. "Doris is only one example," he said. "That is what's happening to thousands and thousands of people in the world."

"I'm afraid you're right," said Fred.

"We've got to do something about it right away!" said Kris with determination.

"You're right, we do," said Fred. "But I wish I knew just what—"

Mr. Kringle was full of ideas. He persuaded Fred to take Doris out to dinner the following evening. Fred was only too eager to ask her, but she had steadfastly refused up to now. This time, Kris convinced him, things would be different. He would see to that.

The next morning Kris gave Doris a great sales talk about her neighbor, Mr. Gayley. Doris seemed to agree with everything he said. He also quite casually mentioned the need for recreation, especially for someone who worked as hard as Doris, and again she agreed.

So when Fred appeared in the Toy Department at closing time, Kris beamed at him happily as he left his dais. Fred had come to take Doris to dinner, hadn't he? Fred shook his head. Mrs. Walker was much too busy, as usual. She was working the whole evening. Her dinner would be a sandwich and coffee at her desk. So Fred had stopped by for Kris. He thought they could go home together.

"Oh, I see," said Mr. Kringle dryly. "She's too busy to see you, eh? Well, perhaps if I talked to her . . ."

"It's no use," Fred told him. "I've talked myself hoarse."

"I see," Kris mused. "We'll have to think of something." There was a peculiar glint in Mr. Kringle's eyes as he retired to the locker room to change.

It seemed to Fred that he took a long time about it, too. Finally he went back to the locker room to find Kris. But the old man had gone. He had taken

49

the service elevator down quite some time ago, the porter told him.

What was Kris up to? Fred decided to return to Doris' office and use the phone. Cleo had not seen him and nobody answered the phone in Fred's apartment. Doris called the Maplewood Home, but he had not been there.

By now Doris had become quite alarmed. Kris had punched his time card and placed it in the rack as usual when he left the store. That had been nearly three hours ago.

But if Kris had met with disaster they could find no trace of it. They checked all the police stations, hospitals, and remembering Mr. Sawyer's dire predictions, Doris, with her heart in her mouth, even called the psychopathic ward at Bellevue. Kris was no place to be found.

As the evening wore on and their search continued, Doris' anxiety grew and it was not based entirely on Mr. Macy and her job. Fred was surprised to find that Doris had grown much fonder of Mr. Kringle than she, herself, realized.

"I'm frankly amazed at you," he told her.

"Why?" asked Doris.

"Well, it's not like you at all," he told her. "The efficient businesslike Mrs. Walker getting so upset about an eccentric old man."

"Kris is not just an eccentric old man, Fred," said Doris. "He's much more than— He's—he's—" Doris couldn't find the words.

"I know just what you mean," said Fred, trying to conceal his elation. But all the efforts gained them nothing. They could find no trace of Mr. Kringle anywhere.

Finally, heartsick and exhausted, Fred took Doris home. On the way they stopped off at the Central Park Zoo, but Jim had not seen Kris since last Sunday when he had brought the little girl. That was their last straw. Now all they could do was wait and hope, and to add to Doris' unhappiness, she had lost a lovely little brooch, a treasured heirloom, and they had been to so many places all through the store, the zoo and in cabs, that she knew she'd never see it again.

When Fred left Doris at the door to her apartment she was on the verge of tears. His heart went out to her, but he knew her too well to say anything that might sound tender or comforting. The evening had brought them closer than they had ever been before but any acknowledgment of this, he knew, would only frighten her right back into her shell again. So he simply said good night and turned to go.

But Doris seemed reluctant to see him leave. She

wanted to thank him for all he'd done. "I—I don't know how I ever could have gone through the evening without you," she said.

Fred smiled quietly. "You see, a man does come in handy every once in a while," he said. "I'm glad I could be helpful."

"You were more than helpful, Fred," she said. "And—and I'm more than grateful."

He could see the tears welling up in her eyes now. She took a little step toward him and raised her head, and for a fleeting second Fred thought she was going to kiss him. But something quickly caught her and held her face frozen into a smile.

"Good night," said Fred softly as he closed the door.

He was still smiling warmly to himself as he entered his dark apartment. If it hadn't been for Kris, it would have been a wonderful evening. He was still puzzled by the old man's disappearance. At first he had felt sure it was some trick that Kris was playing, but as the evening wore on a cold fear had begun to grip his heart. If anything had really happened to Mr. Kringle, the world would never be the same.

As he snapped on the light in his bedroom, Fred suppressed a bellow—for there in his bed lay Mr. Kringle peacefully asleep. Fred quickly snapped off the light again, but Kris was already sitting up eagerly and asking Fred what had happened.

"We nearly went crazy, that's what happened!" Fred told him. "You mean to say you've been here all the time?"

Kris nodded with a chuckle.

"Why didn't you answer the phone?" Fred asked. "We didn't know what had happened to you. Doris and I've been chasing all over town."

"Oh, you have, eh?" said Kris with a twinkle in his eye. "Didn't you enjoy it? Didn't you two get together?"

Well, yes—Fred was forced to admit they had. Kris grinned with satisfaction.

"That's exactly what I hoped would happen! I'll have to try it again!"

"No! No!" Fred pleaded anxiously. There must be easier ways.

"You ought to be ashamed of yourself," Fred told him, trying his best to look angry. "Think of all the worry you caused Doris. I'm going over and tell her what a fiend you are before the poor girl spends a sleepless night!"

"Yes, do, by all means," said Kris, beaming. "That'll give you a little *more* time together!"

Doris came to the door in a sheer, ruffled dressing gown, her hair streaming down her back. Fred had never seen her looking so feminine or appealing before. She seemed to be another person, a soft alluring contrast to the severely tailored Mrs. Walker he had left a few minutes ago. Doris was so relieved by the news he brought that she quite forgot her appearance as she let Fred in. But she couldn't understand it. Why had the old man done it? Where had he gone? Fred tried gingerly to explain.

"It seems Mr. Kringle is playing Cupid as well as Santa Claus," he said. "He thinks we're two nice people and that we should spend more time together."

"Oh!" said Doris. But she didn't seem to mind the idea nearly as much as Fred thought she would.

"That's why he did it. And I'll bet the old fox is peeping at us from his window right now," Fred concluded.

"Well, in that case, you'd better stay and have a cup of coffee," said Doris. Kris could see into her living room from his bedroom, she pointed out. Fred very happily accepted the invitation.

Fred enjoyed the next half hour more than any he could remember—for there was Doris next to him on the couch and his arm was around her. Every time she moved away, Fred suddenly noticed that Kris was peeking at them; of course, half the time Kris wasn't there. Finally Fred could no longer use

Mr. Kringle for an excuse for it was obvious that the old man must have been asleep a long time.

As he rose to leave there came a terrified cry from Susan in her bed. The child was having a nightmare. Fred rushed into her room and caught Susan up in his arms. Doris followed, standing near the doorway. As Fred quietly comforted her, Susan slowly awoke from the dream and as she saw Fred a smile of happiness broke out on her tear-streaked face.

"Oh, Uncle Fred, it's you," she said with great relief and reassurance. She had had an awful dream —but now that Uncle Fred was here everything was all right. Doris was deeply moved by the little scene and strangely touched by her daughter's devotion to "Uncle Fred."

As Fred said good night to Doris he took her tenderly in his arms and kissed her—and neither of them mentioned Mr. Kringle or the act they were supposed to be putting on.

❦ ❦ ❦ 9 ❦ ❦ ❦

FRED boldly entered the imposing portals of Tiffany & Company the following afternoon. He wanted to buy a brooch, he told the elderly dignified clerk who condescended to wait on him. But he wanted a certain kind. He tried to describe the one Doris had lost, without much success. The clerk showed him several very handsome brooches. But none of them seemed to be what Fred was looking for. The clerk finally thought he knew what Fred had in mind. Unfortunately he had nothing like that at the moment.

"Why don't you try Cartier's?" he suggested. "It's only a few blocks away. They have some lovely things."

Fred stared at the clerk in amazement.

"Cartier's sent me here," he said.

"Oh, yes," remarked the clerk, "Cartier's have sent us a number of customers lately."

Fred left the store still lost in wonder. He had seen the advertisements and news stories heralding the wave of good will which Kris had started; but he realized now for the first time how widespread it had become. If Tiffany's were sending people to Cartier's, anything could happen!

Fred finally found a brooch he liked and he entered Macy's in high spirits. To his surprise everyone in the store seemed to reflect his mood. The doorman, a perennially harassed giant, beamed at him pleasantly; the elevator boys wore grins as big as his; even the herd of customers who jammed the aisles seemed to be in a new and jovial mood as they poked each other and trod on each other's toes. Fred's astonishment grew with each new proof of Kris' magic.

Mrs. Walker was not in her office and Kris was not on his dais, but in one corner of the Toy Department a large crowd had gathered. Fred found Doris in the crowd watching what was going on in silent awe. For there in a special setting in front of a Christmas tree stood Mr. Macy and Mr. Gimbel actually shaking hands! They were posing for photographers with Kris beaming behind them.

"This," said Doris, "is the miracle of miracles—a sight I never thought I'd live to see!"

"And it's all because of Mr. Kringle!" Fred mused.

Doris nodded silently and smiled at Fred. Bulbs flashed as Macy and Gimbel faced the battery of cameras, smiling cordially as each pumped the other's hand.

"Now we'll take one over at *my* store," said Mr. Gimbel.

And Mr. Macy eagerly agreed. Doris turned to Fred. "Pinch me, Fred," she said. "I simply don't believe it!"

Doris watched wide-eyed as the formalities proceeded. Now Mr. Macy was formally presenting Kris with a check, a bonus from the Company: "In appreciation of the wonderful new spirit which you have brought not only to Macy's but to the entire city as well!" Mr. Kringle accepted it happily. Mr. Macy jokingly asked him what he intended to do with all that money.

Kris knew exactly what he would do. "I'm going to make this a particularly happy Christmas for someone who has been very kind to me," he said. "He's a doctor and I'm going to give him an X-ray machine!"

"Well," Macy replied, "that's going to be quite expensive!"

"Let me handle it," said Mr. Gimbel eagerly. "We'll get it for you wholesale!"

"*We'll* get it at cost!" said Mr. Macy.

Fred turned to Doris and took a little package from his pocket.

"I have a little presentation to make myself," he said as he handed it to her. "But I thought I'd omit any formal ceremonies."

Doris was touched and delighted by the brooch. She even allowed Fred to pin it on her. As they walked back toward her office, Doris slipped her arm through his. Right in front of the entire Toy Department she was walking with him arm in arm!

To Fred this was even greater than the Macy-Gimbel miracle.

"It seems to me you're catching the Kringle spirit, too," he said.

Doris looked up at him and smiled. "I'm afraid I am," she replied.

❧ ❧ ❧ 10 ❧ ❧ ❧

THAT evening, when the happy triumvirate came home to Doris' apartment, they saw Susan playing with three or four other children. Doris was surprised because up to now Susan had been more or less a lone-wolf cub in the neighborhood, content to amuse herself in her own room. She had always complained that the other children played silly games. But here she was now, knee-deep in a game of fantasy and liking it. Of course, she was not quite as experienced as the other kids in pretending to be a witch, but she was trying, and it was obvious that under Kris' coaching her imagination was developing nicely. Doris couldn't help but be pleased as she watched Susan romp all over the furniture, trying to scare the other witches. Maybe the psychologists would not approve of a six-year-old making believe she was a nonexistent sorceress—but at the moment

Doris did, because she had never seen Susan enjoying herself quite so much.

At dinner, Doris seemed a different person. She was happy, relaxed, warm, and feminine—the exact opposite of the stern Mrs. Walker of a few weeks ago. Kris was in the clouds. As he read a story to Susan after dinner, he glowed happily and assured the child that she would get her wish for Christmas.

In the kitchen, Doris and Fred were helping Cleo with the dishes. Doris regretfully explained to Fred that she had to leave him for the evening. Mr. Sawyer, the vocational guidance expert, was giving a lecture before a study group of personnel heads. Doris was chairman of the committee, she had arranged for Sawyer to speak and was to introduce him. Much as she hated to go, she was afraid she simply had to—the meeting had been planned weeks ago. Due to the nature of the lecture, Doris thought it just as well not to mention where she was going in front of Kris.

After she had gone, Fred and Kris put Susan to bed. While Fred went next door to get his pipe and tobacco, Kris' eye caught a mimeographed postcard lying on Doris' desk. He picked it up and read it:

61

PERSONNEL STUDY GROUP

Doris Walker, Chairman

Will meet at 8:30 P.M., Wed., Dec. 18, in
the Neighborhood Center Auditorium, Greenwich Village
Speaker: MR. ALBERT SAWYER
Subject: EXPLODING THE MYTH OF SANTA CLAUS

An open discussion will follow the lecture.

Kris Kringle's whole being bristled as he read this.
He picked up his hat and his cane and stalked out.

At the Neighborhood Center the usher politely
refused to let Kris into the auditorium. Admission
to the lecture was by invitation only and Kris had
left the card in Doris' apartment. But Mr. Kringle
was determined to hear what this lunkhead Sawyer
had to say. Quietly he decided to do some exploring;
there must be other ways of getting into the place.
He wandered slowly down a hallway which seemed
to run along the side of the auditorium. After a bit
he came to a door which was unlocked. He opened
it quietly and walked up a few steps. As he did so he
heard Doris' voice saying, ". . . and so it gives me
great pleasure to introduce Mr. Albert Sawyer."
There followed a polite round of applause. Kris
found himself back stage.

Sawyer began by saying that the setting in which

62

he found himself seemed hardly appropriate for a lecture of this sort, but he hoped the audience would bear with him. It seemed that the Children's Theater was giving its Christmas production on this stage and the set, which contained a large window and a huge fireplace, could not be removed between performances. Sawyer was at the front of the stage, reading his speech at a lectern.

"The symbolic figure of Santa Claus, St. Nicholas, or Kris Kringle," he began, "represents a classic expression of the wishful dreaming of *all* children. He is the omnipotent Giver, the generous Father. Mature adults who seek to perpetrate this myth reveal themselves as incomplete and neurotic personalities. They are clinging to infantile fantasies and show themselves unable to face reality."

This last remark was greeted with an audible burst of laughter from the audience. Sawyer looked up, disturbed. He did not know that behind him, at the back of the stage, the figure of Kris Kringle was framed in the large cellophane window.

But Doris had spotted Kris, and she was in a panic. She had no idea how he had gotten there, or what he would do next.

Still mystified by the laughter, Sawyer continued with his lecture. People often wished to act as Santa, he said, and this they did to compensate for strong feelings of guilt. Fathers who felt guilty toward their children showered them with gifts, and wealthy men who played Santa by vast philanthropies covered feelings of guilt about the money they had made at the expense of others.

As Sawyer continued, Kris, behind the scenery, began to sputter and fume and shake his cane in anger. Doris anxiously tried to quiet him with grimaces and gestures, but as Sawyer's remarks grew more and more condemning Kris' mutterings grew more and more voluble.

Kris now had but one idea—to get out from behind the scenery onto the stage. He finally saw a small aperture in the backdrop.

At that moment Sawyer dealt a terrific body blow to the whole subject of Santa Claus.

"Far from doing good in the world, this vicious myth has done more harm than opium," he declared.

This last was too much for Mr. Kringle. Before Doris knew what had happened, he had burst out onto the stage. His entrance could not have been more dramatic. Right in the middle of this diatribe against Santa the living image of Santa Claus appeared out of the fireplace.

Kris' entrance was too much for the audience. They rocked and screamed with laughter, but to Mr. Kringle it was not funny.

Sawyer was astounded to see Kris and he was also very angry.

"Now look here . . . !" Kris began.

"*I* am giving this lecture, Mr. Kringle," Sawyer declared.

The name of Kringle brought another laugh which Sawyer had not expected. Doris was on her feet now, vainly pleading with Kris.

"There is to be open discussion," replied Kringle. "I believe I have a right to be heard—I don't know anyone better qualified than myself to answer your absurd remarks."

"The discussion will take place *after* the lecture," said Mr. Sawyer.

"Very well," said Kris. He walked to one side of the stage, seated himself on a prop bench, and waited for Sawyer to resume.

Completely flustered, poor Mr. Sawyer attempted to continue, but Kris was still the center of attention. Each time Sawyer made a remark which seemed ridiculous to Kris, his face clearly indicated his reaction. All Kris had to do was raise one eyebrow or touch his nose with his cane to bring a roar of laughter from the listeners.

It was at this point that Fred slipped into the back of the auditorium. Having exhausted all means of locating Kris, he had found the card on Doris' desk, and rushed here to tell her. When he saw Kris peacefully seated on the platform, he gave a relieved grin and sat down to watch the proceedings.

Sawyer became more and more confused as he struggled to continue. He began to stutter and to mix words up. His reference to "Clanta Sause" sent the audience into stitches, and the more they laughed the worse Sawyer grew. Finally, one sentence came out so garbled that Mr. Sawyer had to start it all over again. Kris could not resist the temptation. He held up two fingers at Mr. Sawyer.

"How many fingers do you see?" he asked.

This was too much for Mr. Sawyer. He turned white with rage.

"I refuse to continue," he stormed, "until this old jackanapes is removed from the platform."

Doris was on her feet, beseeching Kris to be reasonable.

"I am entirely reasonable, my dear," said Kris. "But I intend to show the absurdity of all this hogwash *Mr.* Sawyer has been spouting—and until I do, I'll not move one inch!"

"You won't, eh?" said Sawyer, advancing ominously. "We'll see about that!"

Mr. Kringle held his ground. "Jackanapes, am I?" he said ominously, and he toyed with his cane as Sawyer approached.

66

"Don't you threaten me with that stick!" roared Sawyer. "Leave this platform, do you hear?"

Kris raised his cane, preparing to defend himself, and Sawyer grabbed for it furiously. With a quick tug Mr. Kringle pulled it free. As he did so, the stick grazed Mr. Sawyer's cheek.

"He hit me!" screamed Sawyer, jumping back.

"I wish I had," said Mr. Kringle scornfully. Doris quickly stepped between them, trying to restore order.

"Look here, Mrs. Walker," said Sawyer, nursing a slightly red spot on his cheek, "if you insist upon defending this dangerous maniac—I shall call the police at once!"

"No! No!" cried Doris, anxiously.

Sawyer at last saw his chance to do some face-saving and make an exit. Things had got entirely out of control.

"Ladies and gentlemen," he announced, "the lecture is terminated." He turned to Doris. "Very well, I shall not call the police—now. I will see you in Mr. Shellhammer's office tomorrow morning and we shall decide on a course of action." He glared at Kris. "Society has ways of protecting itself against such people!" And with that he strode from the platform.

❦ ❦ ❦ II ❦ ❦ ❦

EARLY the next morning Doris found herself facing the combined wrath of Messrs. Sawyer and Shellhammer. Sawyer had given a lurid account of Kris' behavior the night before. He had left no doubt but that Kringle was a dangerously deranged man. He accused him of profanity and violence. Doris attempted to refute Sawyer's exaggerations. Kris' appearance at the lecture was unfortunate, but he had not really done anything violent.

Shellhammer was disturbed. Sawyer had convinced him that Kringle was extremely dangerous—after all the publicity and build-up he could easily turn out to be a terrific boomerang to Macy's. Just let Gimbel find out that Macy's Santa was a nut—good grief! They did not dare to imagine the possibilities! Kringle was dynamite, and Mrs. Walker was responsible. She had hired him; she had known about his delusion.

Mr. Sawyer was only thankful that *he* had been the victim instead of one of the innocent little children Kris had dangled on his knee. "The problem," said Sawyer, "is what to do about this—this poor, deluded maniac."

"We've got to do something at once!" said Shellhammer.

"I don't believe it," Mrs. Walker was saying. "He's just a kind old man. I'm sure that he won't ever . . ."

"Oh, but he *will*, Mrs. Walker!" Mr. Sawyer assured her. "He's evidently suffered some sudden change. He's entered into a violent phase."

"But Dr. Pierce assured us that could never happen in this type of case. Kris' delusion is only for good."

"Dr. Pierce is not a psychiatrist," said Sawyer tartly.

"Neither are you," snapped Doris.

"Well, the very least that should be done," said Sawyer, "is to have Mr. Kringle thoroughly examined by competent psychiatrists, at once."

This seemed very sound to Mr. Shellhammer. Doris objected; Kris had passed dozens of such examinations with flying colors, she pointed out.

"But there's no harm in it," Shellhammer argued.

"If they agree with Dr. Pierce that he's harmless, he can come right back."

"And if they *don't*, you've certainly done the right thing," added Sawyer.

Doris was quite shaken. She knew that Kris had not been violent. She disliked Sawyer intensely and she was sure that he was exaggerating the situation. But under the circumstance, Mr. Shellhammer was right, she knew. Anyway, Kris would obviously pass any sanity test with flying colors and he would be back on the job that afternoon. Doris acquiesced with a nod.

Mr. Sawyer was eager and obliging. He would be glad to arrange for the examination right away, he said. His one aim was to get Kringle away from the store as quickly as possible. There was no time to lose. He knew the quickest and easiest way to do it, too. But there was no need to mention that to Mrs. Walker.

"The only problem now," said Sawyer, "is how to get him out of the store without creating another —er—situation. In his present condition, he would most certainly react with violence."

"Mrs. Walker, you'll have to explain it to him," said Shellhammer. "After all, you're his friend. He trusts you."

But Doris flatly refused. She agreed that it must

70

be done, but she simply couldn't do it. She had come to be far too fond of the old man. She couldn't bring herself to hurt him.

"Never mind," said Sawyer with a quiet nod to Shellhammer. "We don't really need Mrs. Walker. I know how we can do it."

Kris was back on his dais as usual greeting the never-ending line of youngsters as Mr. Shellhammer approached him. They wanted to have Mr. Kringle's picture taken with the Mayor down at City Hall. Would Kris mind going?

"Not a bit," said Kris. "I'd be delighted to meet His Honor, but I have a five o'clock appointment with Mr. Macy . . ."

"Oh, you'll be back in plenty of time for that," Mr. Shellhammer assured him. These two gentlemen would take him—a car was waiting—and so Kris left his dais and went with the men.

It was not until he entered the limousine and saw Mr. Sawyer sitting in the front seat that Kris suspected anything.

"Where to?" the driver asked.

"Bellevue," said Sawyer.

Kris started to rise angrily but the car was already in motion and the men on either side of him quietly forced him back into his seat. He sat there stunned and staring straight ahead as the car moved slowly with the traffic down the rain-soaked street. Then he finally spoke.

"Does Mrs. Walker know about this?" he asked.

"Of course she does," said Sawyer. "She arranged the whole thing."

From that minute on Mr. Kringle was a beaten man. If Doris could do this to him, all he had worked so hard for was a lost and hopeless cause. It didn't matter a bit what happened to him now. All the rest of the way to Bellevue he never uttered a word. And even when they arrived and he was taken inside he seemed to have lost all interest in what was going on.

❧ ❧ ❧ 12 ❧ ❧ ❧

FOR Doris the rest of the afternoon was an endless, unreal ordeal of suspense. She couldn't force herself to remain seated at her desk for more than a few minutes at a time, let alone concentrate upon her work. She kept going to the door and looking at the dais hoping to see that Kris had returned. But the dais remained empty and her anxiety increased. She tried to learn where Kris had been taken, but all that Mr. Shellhammer knew was that Mr. Sawyer had arranged for the examination and that he had gone with Mr. Kringle in the car.

It wasn't till nearly closing time that she finally learned the truth. Then she received a hurried and furious telephone call from Fred. He had just hung up from talking to the Psychopathic Ward at Bellevue. They had asked him to bring down Mr. Kringle's toilet articles right away.

"It was some doctor down there," Fred told her

indignantly. "He said Kris wouldn't be needing any street clothes for quite a while!"

"Bellevue! So that's where Sawyer took him—!" Doris' voice was choked with rage.

"What's happened anyway?" Fred demanded. "What's this all about?"

Doris quickly told him the story. Sawyer had made all kinds of threats. She had no choice but to consent to an examination. Sawyer had been too clever to mention Bellevue, of course.

"But why did you let them take him *anywhere?*" demanded Fred. Doris tried to explain. How could she ignore last night? Suppose Sawyer had sent for the police?

But Fred had no time to argue. He had to get to the hospital right away.

"I'll see you later, Doris," he said as he hung up.

At Bellevue, Mr. Kringle had been interviewed, questioned, examined, put through the regular routine. He had moved from one doctor to another and from one room to another in a dull haze of indifference. He had answered questions absently; often said yes to ridiculous questions because he had paid no attention. All he kept saying to himself over and over again was, "How could she have done it?" "How could she have done it?" Sometimes his lips had silently formed the words. The alert young psychiatrists had noted this and made appropriate entry in their reports.

Now they had taken his Santa Claus costume away and substituted a limp gray dressing gown that was much too big for Kris. They had placed him in a long, bare room with iron bars in front of the narrow windows. There were a lot of other men in the room, all clad in shroudlike dressing gowns. But Mr. Kringle was hardly aware of them. He sat in the chair in which a white-coated attendant had placed him and stared blankly at the wall.

He was still sitting there when Fred found him: a little, tired old man with a white beard. All the youthful, eager brightness was gone from his eyes.

"This is a lot of nonsense, Kris," Fred told him. "You're just as sane as anybody and a whole lot saner than most!"

Kris shook his head almost imperceptibly.

"I'll have you out of here in no time," Fred said heartily.

But Kris did not want to be released. Doris had deceived him, just when he had been convinced that she was really beginning to believe in him.

"She must have been just humoring me all the time," he said sadly. "If that's how sane people behave, I'd rather stay in here with the others."

"But Doris had no idea what Sawyer was up to,"

Fred told him. "He threatened to send for the police. She thought he was going to take you to a private doctor."

"I'm glad to know that," said Kris. "But why didn't *she* come to me herself and explain the whole thing?"

"Because she didn't want to hurt you, Kris."

Kris nodded slowly. "Yes, I'm a nice old man and she felt sorry for me."

"It was more than that," said Fred.

But Mr. Kringle shook his head.

"No—she had doubts, Fred. That's why she was only sorry. If *you* had been dragged off here, she would have been furious."

"What if she *did* have doubts?" Fred argued. "She hasn't really believed in anything for years. You're not giving her a fair chance, Kris!"

"It's not just Doris," Kris said. "It's men like Sawyer. He's dishonest, selfish, vicious. Yet he's called normal and I'm not. He's out there and I'm in here. Well, if *he's* normal, *I* don't want to be. I'd rather stay in here!"

"But you can't just think of yourself, Kris. What happens to you matters to a lot of other people. People like me, who believe in you and what you stand for; and people like little Susan who are just beginning to. You can't quit now, Kris. Don't you see?"

Kris thought this over and as he did the light began to come back into his eyes.

"Maybe you're right," he said slowly. "Maybe you're right, at that!"

"Of course I am!" said Fred with great relief. "I knew you wouldn't let us down."

"I should be ashamed of myself!" said Mr. Kringle, the familiar ring back in his voice. "And I am! Maybe we won't win, Fred, but we'll go down swinging!"

"Now you're talking!" Fred said jubilantly as he rose. "Don't you worry, Kris. Just sit tight and I'll have you out of here in no time!"

But it wasn't as easy as Fred had thought. After a number of unsatisfactory interviews, Fred finally managed to see the Chief Psychiatrist, Dr. Rogers. He was a kindly, quiet man. He sent for Kris' file and studied the papers carefully. Fred explained to Dr. Rogers that he had lived with Kris for quite a time. He was, of course, as sane as any man. This whole procedure was ridiculous, merely revenge for personal humiliation on the part of Mr. Sawyer. But Dr. Rogers was quietly unconvinced. He was sorry but he couldn't agree with Fred at all. Mr. Kringle was definitely unbalanced, if not actually dangerous, at least potentially so. Every interview, every test led clearly to this same conclusion: Mr. Kringle's mind was far from normal. Not only could they not release Kris, but on the basis of these reports they would have to file immediate commitment papers.

It was only then that Fred fully realized what had happened. Kris had given wrong answers and failed these tests deliberately! And at the same time Fred realized that it was hopeless to try to convince Dr. Rogers of the truth.

Sawyer had managed to get Mr. Kringle into this place, but Kris himself had carefully blocked any chance of getting out of it. And Fred had promised Kris his freedom! He had talked himself way out on a long, long limb, and now he felt it cracking. He thanked Dr. Rogers and left. He needed time to think. His job was almost impossible and he knew it.

❧ ❧ ❧ 13 ❧ ❧ ❧

JUDGE HENRY X. HARPER sat in his chambers reading over some routine mail and wondering what to get his wife for Christmas. It had been a good year; things had gone well. He would no doubt be re-elected next spring. He thought the Christmas present ought to be a little more elaborate than usual—perhaps a fur coat?

Finley, his clerk, came in. Mr. Mara from the State Attorney-General's office to see His Honor.

"Show him in—show him in!" said His Honor heartily.

Mr. Mara entered smiling, a folder in his hand. He and the Judge were old friends. They exchanged warm greetings.

"Just some routine commitment papers, Your Honor," Mara told him.

He placed them on the desk. His Honor started to leaf the thick file.

"You'll find everything in order, Judge," said Mara. "I've checked them over—the lunacy report's attached—from Bellevue Hospital."

"Bellevue, eh?" said the Judge, reading. "Age unknown. An old man, is he?"

"Very old, Your Honor."

"I suppose I ought to read all this," sighed Harper.

"You can take my word for it, Judge—it's a cut and dried consent proceeding. This fellow calls himself Kris Kringle. He thinks he's Santa Claus!"

"Oh, oh," His Honor exclaimed with a chuckle. He reached for his pen. As he did so, Finley entered again.

"A Mr. Gayley to see you."

"What does he want?" asked the Judge.

"He's an attorney. It's about this Kringle case."

"Better show him in," sighed the Judge and put his pen down again.

Fred was polite but emphatic. He represented Mr. Kringle, the subject of these papers. In his opinion his client was being railroaded. He requested a proper hearing at which he could bring witnesses.

"I thought you said this was cut and dried?" said the Judge to Mara.

"So I did," said Mara. "This is the first I knew about a protest."

The Judge glanced at the papers again. "Your Honor may sign them if you wish," said Fred, "but I shall bring in a habeas corpus in the morning."

"That won't be necessary," said Judge Harper. "We'll have a hearing. Ten o'clock Monday morning."

Outside in the Judge's anteroom, Mr. Sawyer sat fidgeting nervously, waiting to see Mr. Mara. For Mr. Macy had soon learned of Kris' absence and he had quickly gone into the reasons for it. After interviewing Doris he had called in Mr. Sawyer; and the exact words Macy had used were still ringing in Sawyer's ears. If he didn't succeed in getting Mr. Kringle released immediately, Mr. Sawyer himself would be without a vocation. His career at Macy's would be ended, and just before the Christmas bonus, too!

As Mr. Sawyer sat there trying to keep from biting his nails, Fred emerged from the Judge's chambers and left with a nod to Finley.

"Who—who was that?" asked Sawyer anxiously.

"Mr. Kringle's lawyer," Finley told him. So Kris had a lawyer now! Sawyer didn't like the sound of that at all.

"I'd like to drop the whole case right now," he said when Mara finally appeared.

But Mr. Mara shook his head. "This Kringle's

been committed by a city hospital. It has to go through the regular routine now." Sawyer was petrified.

"Isn't there anything we can do?" he asked.

"Not a thing," said Mara. "There'll be a hearing Monday morning."

A public hearing! It was getting worse and worse, thought Sawyer. He asked about Mr. Kringle's lawyer.

"Oh, that's nothing to worry about at all!" Mara assured him. "This Gayley's just a young punk lawyer trying to get himself a little free publicity!"

Publicity! The word electrified Sawyer. Articles in the newspapers! That was the worst thing that could possibly happen.

"I'd better talk to Mr. Gayley right away!" he said as he dashed off down the hall.

Sawyer caught Fred just as he was getting in the elevator. He introduced himself as Mr. Macy's representative. They were very anxious to avoid any publicity. If Mr. Gayley would co-operate, Mr. Macy would find some very generous way of expressing his appreciation.

Fred laughed quietly. Mr. Macy had nothing to do with this at all and both of them knew it. Mr. Sawyer had placed himself in this frying pan and now he was squirming and wriggling to get out.

"But that publicity idea," said Fred. "I'm glad you mentioned that. I'm going to need all the public opinion I can get to win this case! And publicity's just the way to get it! Much obliged, Mr. Sawyer!"

And he walked away.

The last Mr. Sawyer saw of him was when he entered the Court Reporters' Room. Mr. Sawyer was even more unhappy over that.

The next morning prominent items appeared in most of the New York newspapers. The story was a natural, of course. Kris had become a celebrity; a nationwide symbol of good will. And now he was charged with lunacy. The hearing was front-page news. The evening papers carried even longer stories. The tenor of all the comments was the same. A radio commentator summed it up rather concisely:

"These are strange times," he said. "Kris Kringle, the little Santa Claus who alone is responsible for the wave of good will which has swept this city, and even most of the country, is in trouble! Monday morning, ladies and gentlemen, this simple, kindly old man will appear before Judge Henry X. Harper. And he is charged with, of all things, *lunacy!* Incredible as it may seem, my friends, that is the fact. If bringing back the true Christmas spirit is a form of insanity, then these are very strange times, indeed!"

At his home, Judge Harper heard the broadcast and beamed. His name was on the air from coast to coast! But Charlie Halloran, who was listening with him, wasn't pleased at all. Charlie was the treasurer of the political party which had put the Judge in office. Not an office holder himself, Halloran was a potent power behind many thrones in the state and city, an astute politician and a lifelong friend and advisor of Harper.

"You look kinda rundown to me, Henry," he said thoughtfully. "I think you ought to take a few weeks off."

"Nonsense!" replied His Honor, indignantly. "Never felt better in my life!"

"Go fishing—go hunting—go anywhere," urged Halloran.

"Why should I, Charlie?"

"Because this case is dynamite, Henry," said Charlie as he switched off the radio. "You've got to get out of it some way."

But Henry couldn't. It was all arranged. Then he'd better have a sudden illness, said Charlie. Let some other Judge handle it, somebody who wasn't coming up for re-election in the spring. But His Honor was an honest man. He couldn't do a thing like that, nor did he see why Charlie should be so upset. What was the matter with getting all this good publicity?

"Good!" exclaimed Charlie. "It's terrible! You're a regular Pontius Pilate before you start! You'll be every little kid's villain, and their parents will hate you too!"

"Nonsense," laughed Harper.

At that moment, Mrs. Harper came into the room, calling her grandchildren to come and say good night. She had promised their mother they would be in bed by eight and it was way past that already.

The children came scampering into the room and gave their Granny a big hug and a good night kiss. Then they walked coldly past Judge Harper and up to bed.

The Judge stood there dumbfounded.

"A fine way to treat their grandfather!" he said indignantly.

"I don't blame them!" said Mrs. Harper as she started after the children. "Any man who'll put Santa Claus on trial for lunacy—!"

"You see what I mean," said Charlie, drily—and Judge Harper began to wonder.

❧ ❧ ❧ 14 ❧ ❧ ❧

THE large courtroom was packed with reporters, photographers, columnists, sob-sisters, and a large slice of the general public which was avidly interested in the case.

Mr. Mara, the State's Attorney, slouched in his chair, sorry that he had ever been handed the case. It would be one of those dragged-out affairs. The publicity-seeking lawyer who opposed him would see to that. Kringle would now deny that he ever said he was Santa Claus. Witnesses would have to be called; depositions taken. And only four shopping days left until Christmas. Mara was disgusted.

Now the bailiff chanted his familiar "Hear ye— Hear ye" as Judge Harper entered. Mara rose to open the case.

The lunacy report had already been submitted in evidence. He now wished to call his first witness. Would Mr. Kringle please take the stand?

Kris rose from the table where he had been seated next to Fred and entered the witness box. His Honor studied the old man and he wondered to himself. Mr. Kringle certainly didn't fit the description of the senile old dolt in the report.

"Good morning, Your Honor!" said Mr. Kringle, beaming brightly. In spite of himself, Judge Harper smiled and nodded in return.

"What is your name?" asked Mara.

"Kris Kringle."

"Where do you live?"

"That's what this hearing will decide."

This brought a chuckle from the courtroom and a scowl from Mr. Mara.

"A very sound answer, Mr. Kringle," said His Honor with evident satisfaction.

"Do you believe that you are Santa Claus?"

"Of course!" said Mr. Kringle.

A stunned silence fell over the courtroom. Judge Harper's face fell a long mile. Even Mara was astonished. Why, the old man was admitting his insanity! As far as the State of New York was concerned, the hearing was over. Mara turned to the Judge.

"The State rests, Your Honor," he said dramatically and sat down.

The whole courtroom reacted with excitement.

His Honor was chagrined. He glanced nervously at Charlie Halloran, seated in the crowd. Good grief!—It looked as if he would *have* to declare the old man insane! Halloran returned his glance, shaking his head sadly, telling Henry, "I told you so."

Fred was on his feet now but he seemed not a bit perturbed. He must be a little off the beam, too, thought the Judge to himself.

"Well, young man, don't you want to cross-question the witness? I believe he was employed to *play* Santa Claus," said Harper hopefully, grasping at a straw. "Perhaps he didn't understand the question!"

"I understood it perfectly, Your Honor," said Kris.

"In view of the witness's statement, do you still wish to put in a defense, young man?" His Honor asked dejectedly, as Kris left the stand.

"I do, Your Honor," said Fred. "I am fully aware of the fact that Mr. Kringle believes himself to be Santa Claus. In fact that is the basis of the entire case against him. The State declares that this man is not sane because he believes himself to be Santa Claus."

"I'm afraid that's entirely reasonable and logical," said Judge Harper glumly.

88

"It would be, Your Honor, if you or I or Mr. Mara here believed that we were Santa Claus."

"*Anyone* who thinks he's Santa Claus is insane!" said Mara tartly.

"Not necessarily," said Fred quietly. "You believe yourself to be Judge Harper, and nobody questions your sanity, Your Honor, because you *are* Judge Harper."

The Judge suspected a veiled insult in all this.

"I know all about myself, young man," he said sharply. "Mr. Kringle is the subject of this hearing. Do you still believe that you can show him to be sane?"

"I do," said Fred. "If he is the person he believes himself to be, just as you are, then he is just as sane."

"Of course," said the Judge, "but he isn't."

"Oh, but he *is*, Your Honor!"

"Is *what?*" roared the Judge.

"I intend to prove that Mr. Kringle *is* Santa Claus."

The reaction was instantaneous. This was one of the strangest defenses in legal history. How could this bland young lawyer hope to prove that Kris was Santa Claus himself? It was crazy, but it was good copy. Flash bulbs exploded. Reporters dashed out to reach their phones. There was bedlam in the room. Judge Harper banged his gavel vainly and adjourned the court, but nobody except the court stenographer ever heard him.

There were big stories in all the evening papers. Doris read them on her way home. She was worried. Fred was making a fool of himself, fighting a hopeless battle and jeopardizing his job with his law firm. She wished he had never started the whole business.

When Fred came over that evening she told him so. But Fred was rather confident. All the publicity was working for him, he said. Public sympathy was very obviously behind Kris. It wouldn't be easy but he thought he had a chance. But what about the law firm? What about his job, Doris wanted to know.

Well, Doris was right, it seemed. Old Haislip, the senior member of the firm, had called him in that afternoon. They were an old established firm with great prestige and dignity. They couldn't have one of their junior partners making a public spectacle of himself, trying to prove that some old crank was Santa Claus. Unless he dropped the case at once they would be forced to drop him.

"Well then, you'll have to give it up," said Doris.

"Oh, no, I won't," said Fred. "I can't now, Doris.

You know that. Kris needs me. I can't let the old man down!"

"But what about your job? You can't give *that* up!"

"Well, as a matter of fact, I have already," said Fred. "I told old Mr. Haislip I had no intention of dropping the case. And that was that!"

Now Doris was really upset. How could Fred be so quixotic? People had to be realistic about life. She had learned that. They couldn't go giving up good jobs for any sentimental whim. Fred had asked her to marry him. She had accepted happily. She loved and respected him.

"But when you do a crazy thing like this—well—I thought you were sensible and reliable; not a—a star gazer."

"I guess I am a star gazer. But I'm a darn good lawyer, too! I combine the best features of both," said Fred. "I'll make out all right." But Doris doubted it. She doubted if he'd ever get a job again.

"Well," said Fred, "it all boils down to this: You don't have faith in me."

"Of course I do, but—"

"No, you don't," Fred interrupted. "Not really. You're a very factual person. You don't believe anything unless you've got proof."

"It's not a question of having faith in you. You're bound to lose this case—that's just common sense!"

Fred rose quickly.

"Faith is believing in things when common sense tells you not to," he replied. "And you've just got too much common sense."

"It's a good thing one of us has," said Doris heatedly. "It's rather an asset sometimes!"

"Can't you get over being afraid?" Fred pleaded. "Can't you let yourself believe in people like Kris— in fun and joy and love and all the other intangibles?"

Doris stiffened almost imperceptibly. She became the crisp, efficient Mrs. Walker again.

"You can't pay the rent with intangibles," she said.

"And you can't live a life without them," Fred answered heatedly. "At least, I can't. I thought Kris and I had changed you, Doris. I hoped you'd be ready to string along with me, but—I guess you're not."

Doris turned away silently. Fred gave a hopeless shrug.

"Well, I can see there's no use talking," he said. "We don't even speak the same language, do we? It's just no go, that's all."

Doris stood rigidly, her back to Fred.

"No, I suppose not," she said slowly.

"Then there's nothing more to say."

"No."

Fred picked up his hat and coat in silence. Then Doris turned with a bitter little smile.

"It's funny," she said, "but with all my common sense, I thought it was really going to work out this time."

"So did I," said Fred. He hesitated at the door. Then, "Good night," he said and left.

❦ ❦ ❦ 15 ❦ ❦ ❦

THE next day the hearing was held in an even larger courtroom, and that was packed long before His Honor made his entrance. Most of the crowd was rooting for Kris. The rest were there to see what this crazy young lawyer was going to do. The hearing had caught the public fancy. Judge Harper could have filled the Polo Grounds, had he wished to hold court there.

Fred's first witness was Mr. R. H. Macy. He seemed rather uneasy as he took the oath.

"Are you the owner of one of the largest department stores in New York City?" Fred asked him.

"*The* largest!" said Mr. Macy. He then identified Mr. Kringle as his employee. Did he believe him to be sane? Yes. Did he believe him to be truthful? Yes.

Mr. Mara jumped up.

"Mr. Macy, you are under oath," he warned.

"Do you honestly believe that this man is Santa Claus?"

Mr. Macy hesitated—gulped. But he quickly realized his alternative: If Kris wasn't really Santa Claus, then Macy's Santa was insane. He had no choice:

"Yes!" he said in a loud, defiant voice.

"That is all," said Fred.

On his way back to his seat, Mr. Macy's eye caught Mr. Sawyer seated in the third row. He slackened his brisk pace slightly and glared at Sawyer. "You're fired!" he said, with satisfaction, and moved on quickly up the aisle.

Dr. Pierce was the next to take the stand. He was the physician at the Maplewood Home. He had known Kris for many years. Did he believe him to be Santa Claus?

"I do," said Dr. Pierce quietly.

Again Mara was on his feet. The Doctor was a man of science, was he not? Had he any rational, scientific reason for this opinion? The question was a boomerang for Mara.

"Yes," said Dr. Pierce, "I have."

Mr. Mara sat down. Now Fred questioned Dr. Pierce.

"Did you express a wish for Christmas to Mr. Kringle several weeks ago?"

"Yes," said Dr. Pierce. What was it? "Well, I wanted an X-ray machine for the Home." Had he expressed this wish to anyone else? "No—it was too fantastic. X-ray equipment is very expensive." What had arrived at the Maplewood Home the day before? "The X-ray machine," said the Doctor. Where had it come from? "The card said 'Merry Christmas from Kris Kringle.'" Did he know of any other possible donor? "No." What did he conclude from this?

"Well," said Dr. Pierce, "when I made the wish I said to myself—if I really get this X-ray machine, I'll believe he's Santa Claus. It came and so I do."

Next Fred put Jim, the zoo keeper, on the stand. Jim testified to Mr. Kringle's uncanny way with reindeer. He, their keeper, could only come near them when they were tied, and he had fed them for twelve years. Yet these same reindeer walked right up to Mr. Kringle and ate out of his hand!

This was too much for Mr. Mara. He objected to the whole line of testimony. It was ridiculous, ir- relevant, and immaterial. Mr. Gayley was making a circus out of this court. There was no such person as Santa Claus and everybody knew it. There was a murmur of disagreement from the courtroom. Fred said that was purely a matter of opinion. Could

Mr. Mara offer any proof that there was *no* Santa Claus?

Mr. Mara grew hot under the collar. No, of course he couldn't, and he didn't intend to! This was no nursery. This was a New York State Supreme Court! They were only wasting the court's time with this childish nonsense. Was there or was there not a Santa Claus? He asked the Judge for an immediate ruling.

His Honor looked very unhappy, indeed. Mara had won, he feared. Officially he could make but one decision. Then his eye fell on Charlie Halloran among the spectators. Charlie was shaking his head violently and gesturing toward the Judge's chambers.

"The court will take a short recess to consider the matter," announced the Judge.

"Look," said Charlie when they were alone, "I don't care what you decide about old whisker-puss out there. But if you go back and officially rule that there's no Santa Claus, you might as well start looking for that chicken farm right now. We can't even put you up for the primaries."

"But how can I say there *is* a Santa Claus, Charlie? I'm a responsible judge. I've taken an oath. If I do they'll have me disrobed. They'll try *me* for insanity!"

"Listen, Henry," said Charlie, trying to control himself. "Do you know how many millions of dollars' worth of toys are made each year? Toys that wouldn't be sold if it weren't for Santa Claus? Have you ever heard of the National Association of Manufacturers? How do you think they'll like your ruling? And what about all the men they employ to make these toys? Union men! What about the A.F. of L. and the C.I.O.? They're gonna love you, Henry! And they're gonna say it with votes! Then there are the department stores. And the candy companies, and the Christmas card makers, and the Salvation Army. They've got a Santa Claus on every corner. You're gonna be an awful popular feller, Henry! And what about the Christmas baskets *we* give out? Henry, I'm telling you—if you rule that there's no Santa Claus you can count on getting just two votes—yours and that fellow Mara's."

His Honor shook his head sadly and raised one finger.

"Mara's a Republican," he said.

His Honor returned to the bench with dignity and called the court to order.

"The question of Santa Claus," he found, "is by and large a matter of opinion. Many people firmly believe in him. Many others do not. The tradition of American justice demands a broad and unprejudiced view of such a controversial matter. This court intends to keep an open mind. It will hear any evidence on either side."

Suppressed cheers greeted this announcement. Mr. Mara looked at Fred scornfully. Could he produce any such evidence? Yes, Fred could. Would Mr. Thomas Mara please take the stand?

"Who, me?" said Mara, startled.

Fred shook his head.

"Thomas Mara, *Junior*," he said.

A seven-year-old boy left his mother and came dashing down the aisle. Mr. Mara was completely bewildered at the sudden appearance of his son. He glared angrily at his wife standing near an aisle seat. She held up a subpoena and shook her head in a gesture of helpless innocence. By the time Mara had regained his composure, Tommy was eagerly beginning to testify.

"Do you believe in Santa Claus?" Fred was asking him.

"Sure I do. He gave me a brand-new sled last year!"

"What does he look like, Tommy?"

Tommy pointed unerringly at Mr. Kringle.

"There he is sitting right there!"

Mr. Mara protested feebly.

"Overruled," said His Honor sternly.

"Tell me, Tommy, why are you so sure there is a Santa Claus?" asked Fred.

"Because my Daddy told me so!" said Thomas, Jr., indicating his father. A roar of laughter came from the crowd. Even the Judge was grinning broadly as he rapped for order.

"And you believe your Daddy, don't you, Tommy? He's a truthful man."

Thomas was very indignant at this foolish question.

"Of course he is. My Daddy wouldn't tell me a thing that wasn't so!"

"Thank you, Tommy," said Fred quietly, and sat down.

The crowd reacted again. Thomas Mara, Senior, rose to his feet, filled with confusion. Tommy scrambled down from the witness box and started for his mother. On the way he passed close to Mr. Kringle. The temptation was irresistible. He leaned over to Kris confidentially.

"Don't forget!" he said, in a loud stage whisper. "A real offishill football helmet!"

"You shall have it, Tommy," Kris told him, beaming. And Tommy ran happily back to his mother.

Mr. Mara glanced quickly toward his son and then back to the Judge.

"Your honor," he said slowly, "the State of New York concedes the existence of Santa Claus."

"This court concurs," said Judge Harper happily. He had gotten out of that one nicely. He beamed at Charlie in the crowd and Charlie winked and smiled approvingly.

Fred had made tremendous progress, far beyond his wildest hopes, but he still had the major hurdle ahead of him, and he knew it. And what was far worse, Mara knew it too.

"But having so conceded, Your Honor," Mara was saying, "we ask that Mr. Gayley cease presenting personal opinion as evidence. The State could bring in hundreds of witnesses with opposite opinions. But it is our desire to shorten this hearing rather than prolong it. I therefore demand that Mr. Gayley now submit *authoritative proof* that Mr. Kringle is *the one and only Santa Claus!*"

"Your point is well taken, Mr. Mara," the Judge said. "I'm afraid I must agree."

Was Mr. Gayley prepared to show that Kringle was Santa Claus on the basis of competent authority?

Fred was not prepared to do so at this time. He asked for an adjournment.

"This hearing stands adjourned till tomorrow afternoon at three!" announced the Judge quickly.

Fred left the courtroom with a heavy heart. He was afraid that he was licked. What "competent authority" could he possibly produce? It looked as if the case of Mr. Kringle were a lost cause.

✤ ✤ ✤ 16 ✤ ✤ ✤

WHEN Doris came home that evening, Susan's first question was, "Is Mr. Kringle coming over tonight?"

Doris was afraid not.

"He hasn't been here for so long," said Susan. "Won't he come soon, Mother?"

Doris had read the newspaper account of the day's events at the trial. The reporters were rooting hard for Mr. Kringle, but the outcome seemed inevitable.

"Susan, Mr. Kringle may never be able to come here again," she said.

"Why not?"

"Well," Doris tried to explain, "it's because he says he's Santa Claus."

"But he *is* Santa, Mother—I know he is."

"Some people don't believe that, Susan. So they're having sort of a trial."

"But he *must* be Santa Claus," said Susan. "He's

so sweet and kind and jolly, and nobody could be like Mr. Kringle except Santa Claus."

"I think perhaps you're right," said Doris.

"Is Mr. Kringle unhappy, Mother?"

"I'm afraid he is, dear," Doris answered.

"Then I'm going to write him a letter right away to cheer him up!" Susan would not eat her supper until she had completed the letter.

After supper Doris helped her address the envelope to Mr. Kris Kringle, New York County Court House, Center and Pearl Streets, New York City. Susan rushed off to finish the game in another child's apartment. Doris promised to mail the letter right away. She read it over smiling:

DEAR MR. KRINGLE,

I MISS YOU VERY MUCH AND I HOPE I WILL SEE YOU SOON. I KNOW IT WILL COME OUT ALL RIGHT. I BELIEVE YOU ARE SANTA CLAUS AND I HOPE YOU ARE NOT SAD.   YOURS TRULY,

SUSAN WALKER.

Doris stood there thoughtfully a second. Then she added a footnote: "I believe in you, too," and signed it "Doris." Quickly she sealed the envelope and stamped it Special Delivery. Then she walked out into the hall and dropped it into the mail chute.

Down at the main post office late that night, Al Golden was sorting the mail. Under his visor he was scowling as he viciously chewed at his cigar. Christmas was wonderful; Al had kiddies, too. But Christmas mail was a big pain in the neck. It wasn't only the extra packages and letters—it was those letters to Santa Claus. There were literally thousands of them. They had bags and bags of it cluttering up the place. It had to be kept for thirty days, too—some crazy old law. Suddenly Al stopped sorting and held a letter in his hand.

"Here's a new one!" he said as he picked up Susan's letter. "I've seen 'em write to Santa Claus at the North Pole, the South Pole, care of the Postmaster and every other way. But this kid writes to Mr. Kris Kringle, New York County Court House! Special Delivery, too. Can you beat that?"

"Sure, the kid's right! That's where he is, too," said Lou Spoletti, who was working next to Al. "Don't you read the papers?"

Sure Al read the papers. Lopez had kayoed Garcia in the seventh.

"They got him on trial down there, this Kringle

guy," said Lou. "He claims he's Santa Claus and some D.A. claims he's nuts."

Al looked very thoughtful as he threw Susan's letter in the downtown special delivery bag.

"You mean there's a guy who really might be Santa Claus?" he asked.

"A lot of guys think he is," said Lou, nodding.

"Well, what's the matter with you, Lou?" said Al. "You ain't very bright or somethin'. This guy Kringle's the answer to our prayers!"

"Jeez!" said Lou. "Why didn't I think of that!"

"Order a special big truck—order a couple of 'em," said Al. "Get 'em up here right away! All the Santa Claus mail we got laying around here goes to Mr. Kris Kringle down at the Court House!"

❦ ❦ ❦ 17 ❦ ❦ ❦

IN the Judge's chambers the following afternoon Charlie Halloran was at His Honor again. The publicity on the Kringle hearing had reached unheard-of heights. "Why, they're writin' big headlines about it!"

"I've read the papers, too," said Harper drily.

But what could he do? He had his position to think of—his duty toward his office. Charlie didn't care how he did it—he *had* to set Kringle free.

"Today is Christmas Eve, Henry, and if you sentence Santa Claus to a padded cell on Christmas Eve, you're liable to be picketed—or mobbed—or murdered!"

The Judge was really desperate now. If that Gayley boy could only figure out the slightest possible pretext of "competent authority" the Judge was willing and eager to give him every break. He had observed Mr. Kringle very carefully. He seemed to be nothing worse than a very kindly old gentleman. But unless something miraculous happened he would have to accept the lunacy report and have the old man put away. Judge Harper put on his robe and entered the court.

Fred was deeply worried as the trial resumed. The courtroom had grown tense, as if all present realized that the finale was at hand. Before long it would be Christmas Eve. In a few hours Santa would be starting on his annual ride over the roof-tops, or else. Fred had told Kris that he had tried desperately to obtain competent authority. He had wired the Mayor, the Governor, and many other officials, all to no avail.

Mr. Mara was reading reports from various state institutions and mental hospitals. One had four men who thought they were Napoleon; two who thought they were Caruso; one who thought he was Tarzan. It was clear, Mara pointed out, that delusions like Mr. Kringle's were not uncommon.

This evidence was very damaging indeed. Judge Harper's face grew longer and longer as the trial proceeded. Everyone looked glum except Mr. Kringle. He was even merrier than usual. The reason was Susan's special delivery letter. It had been delivered to him just as the court had reconvened. He read it over and over again. No matter how this hearing ended, he thought, his efforts had not been in vain.

Mara continued reading his reports, submitting them in evidence one after the other. Fred sat there only half listening, desperately trying to figure out something. He was interrupted by a sharp tap on the shoulder. He looked up in surprise. It was one of the uniformed court attendants. He whispered into Fred's ear. Fred looked puzzled and followed the attendant out of the courtroom.

Mara was still droning on as Fred returned to his seat. Kris looked at him in surprise. His manner had suddenly changed. He sneaked a confident wink to Kris. Finally Mara finished. His Honor turned to Fred.

"Have you any further evidence to submit, Mr. Gayley?" he asked in the tone of one who knew the answer.

"I have, Your Honor," said Fred, rising. He held a World Almanac in his hand. "It concerns the Post Office Department, an official agency of the United States Government. The Post Office Department was created July 26, 1776, by the 2nd Continental Congress. The first Postmaster-General was Benjamin Franklin. At the present time the Post Office Department represents one of the largest business organizations in the world. Last year it did a gross business of $1,112,877,174.48. In the last quarter alone it made a net profit of $51,102,-579.64."

Mr. Mara's patience was wearing thin.

"It is indeed gratifying to know that the Post Office Department is doing so nicely," he said, "but it hardly has any bearing on this case."

"It has a great deal of bearing, Your Honor," said Fred. "If I may be allowed to proceed—"

"By all means," said Judge Harper, grasping at any straw.

"The figures I have quoted," said Fred, "indicate an efficiently run organization. Moreover, it has been an official branch of the Federal Government since twenty-two days after the Declaration of Independence. All jobs are under Civil Service. Promotions are strictly on merit. Furthermore, U. S. Postal Laws and Regulations make it a prison offense to deliver mail to the wrong party." He listed a number of safeguards and forms used by the Department to assure the correct and efficient delivery of the mail.

Mr. Mara now rose to protest. This hearing had dragged on long enough.

"Your Honor," he said, "the State of New York is second to none in its admiration of the Post Office

Department. We are ready to concede that it's a most authoritative and efficient organization!"

"For the record?" Fred asked.

"Yes, for the record," said Mara irritably. "Anything to get on with this hearing!"

Then Fred wished to introduce three pieces of evidence. From the Almanac he took three letters and handed them to the Judge. "Mark them Exhibits A, B, and C," he told the clerk. The letters were addressed to: "Santa Claus, U. S. A."—in a childish handwriting.

"These letters," said Fred, "have just now been delivered to Mr. Kringle here in this building by the Post Office Department. I submit, Your Honor, that this is positive proof that a competent Federal authority recognizes Mr. Kringle to be the one and only Santa Claus."

The Judge took the letters and glanced at them. He was very much impressed. Mr. Mara was not. "Three letters," he said, "are hardly positive proof. I understand the Post Office receives thousands of such letters every year."

"I have further exhibits," Fred informed His Honor, "but I hesitate to produce them."

Judge Harper was impatient. The boy had something here.

"Just bring them in, young man! Put them right here on the bench."

"Yes, we'd all like to see them, I'm sure," added Mara. His voice was rich with sarcasm.

"But, Your Honor—" Fred began again.

"I said put them right here!" ordered the Judge.

"Very well, Your Honor," said Fred, and nodded toward a door.

A long line of attendants came in wheeling hand trucks loaded with bags of mail. One by one, they brought them forward, inside the railing, and dumped them before the Judge's bench. The courtroom watched the pile grow until the Judge's bench was almost overwhelmed by an avalanche of letters.

"Your Honor," said Fred, "every one of these is simply addressed: *Santa Claus.*"

His Honor looked up from the pile and banged his gavel.

"The United States of America believes this man is Santa Claus. This court will not dispute it—case dismissed!"

Kris stood up. He was smiling happily, but there were also tears in his eyes. Suddenly he grabbed his hat and coat and cane and dashed up to the bench.

"Thank you, Your Honor," he said, his voice

choked with emotion, "and a Merry Christmas to you."

Judge Harper was beaming broadly.

"A Merry Christmas to you, Mr. Kringle!" he said, extending his hand.

His Honor cast a quick glance out at Charlie Halloran. Charlie was chewing away at his cigar contentedly. He gave the Judge a happy wink.

In the wild excitement which followed Fred was surrounded by admirers, photographed, slapped on the back and congratulated—but he could not find Kris anywhere. The reporters wanted the old man too—they wanted pictures of the one and only—*the* authentic Santa Claus himself. But Mr. Kringle had disappeared.

"Well," said one of the reporters, "it's 5:00 P.M. on Christmas Eve. The old boy couldn't be hanging around here. I'll bet he's hitching up the reindeer now!"

"And it's just beginning to snow too," said another.

In the back of the courtroom Doris rose with the rest of the spectators. She had just slipped in to hear the outcome of the trial. Now she started for the door—then hesitated. Perhaps she ought to offer a word of congratulations to Fred. As she stood there a couple of reporters passed her. One was handing the other a ten-dollar bill.

"Here you are," said the first one, shaking his head. "I never thought he'd pull it off. That letter gag was clever."

"It wasn't just the letters," replied the other reporter. "You've got to hand it to that guy Gayley. He believed in the old man right from the start— and before he was finished he had everybody else believing in him too."

The point hit home. Doris left the courtroom silently. By now everybody was headed for the door —all except the clerk who was trying to extricate himself from the mountain of letters—letters that were there only because a little girl had believed in Mr. Kringle and had written him a note to tell him so.

On his way out Mr. Mara mused over what had happened. He knew he should be filled with anger and defeat, but for some reason or other he wasn't. He actually felt rather gay and cheerful. A sudden thought struck him; he hurried ahead, glancing at his wrist watch.

"Good Lord!" he said anxiously. "I've got to get that football helmet!"

❧ ❧ ❧ 18 ❧ ❧ ❧

ON Christmas morning, bright and early, Susan tiptoed into the living room to see the presents under the tree. There were lots of them too—very exciting-looking packages—but not *the* present—not the one that Kris had promised her. Naturally she hadn't expected to find a house under the tree but she expected some sign or something from Santa to show that her wish was answered. But there was nothing; Mr. Kringle had let her down. Doris came in to find her daughter in tears. Susan's disappointment was bitter. Mr. Kringle wasn't really Santa Claus after all!

Doris took Susan in her arms to comfort her but the child pulled away. Her mother had always told her there was no Santa Claus and she was right—Susan could see that now. The whole business was a lot of silly nonsense. As she listened, Doris could almost hear herself—and it wasn't pleasant.

"I was wrong when I told you that," Doris said. "You *must* believe in Mr. Kringle—and keep on believing. You must have faith in him."

But how could you believe that a poor old man who worked in a store was really Santa and would give you your Christmas wish?

"Faith is believing in things when common sense tells you not to," said Doris, echoing Fred's words as much to herself as to Susan. The child didn't quite understand, so Doris went on. If you didn't believe you never would get the things you really wanted. Doris had learned that, to her bitter sorrow. Anyone could have faith when everything was fine. But real faith meant believing, rain or shine. She reminded Susan of her letter and how her belief had encouraged Doris. Now the tables were turned—and Susan must believe, too.

Susan thought it over for a moment and then began muttering with firm conviction: "I believe, I believe, I believe—"

The annual Christmas morning breakfast at the Maplewood Home was to be especially festive this year—for Mr. Kringle was coming back! The hero of the hour—legally declared sane and therefore eligible to return. Even the Board of Directors were on hand to greet him. But Kris had failed to make his appearance and people were beginning to fidget. Dr. Pierce was phoning everyone he could think of, including Jim, the keeper at the zoo. No sign of Kris, said Jim, looking out in the yard. But what was even worse—no sign of the reindeer either! When he had hung up, Jim made a wild dash for their shed and then stopped in amazement. There were his reindeer sitting down in pairs, panting, their bodies covered with sweat and lather. Jim shook his head.

A few minutes later Kris came walking briskly into Maplewood. He seemed tired but full of good cheer. The greetings were effusive. They were waiting for him to officiate under the Christmas tree as he had for so many years. But before he could do that Mr. Kringle had to make a call—he wanted to invite some special guests—if it was all right.

Kris called Fred and asked him to do him a special favor. Would he get Doris and Susan and bring them out here? "Well," said Fred, "you know how things are, Kris."

"I know," said Kris, "but on Christmas morning—" So of course Fred agreed. Kris, it seemed, had gotten about quite a bit that night—he seemed to have very recent knowledge of the conditions of all the roads. He outlined a route for Fred to take.

The snowstorm had been quite severe—he had better follow Kris's instructions.

Fred, with some embarrassment, rang Doris's doorbell. He explained that Kris had called. Were they willing to go with him? Doris's manner was also strained. She tried to be casual in front of Susan but it was difficult. Of course they would be glad to go.

It was a beautiful Christmas morning. The countryside was glistening and white under the brand new layer of snow. The rather roundabout way which Kris had recommended led through pleasant suburban streets. Each house had a gay Christmas wreath in the window and one on the door.

Suddenly Susan gave a cry and nearly jumped right through the window of the car. There was her house—her Christmas present. They must stop at once! Fred and Doris looked at each other in bewilderment as he brought the car to a stop.

Susan was beside herself with excitement as she ran up the walk. She *knew* this was her house! It was exactly like the picture—the picture she had given Mr. Kringle! With complete assurance Susan opened the door and went inside. Fred and Doris followed silently, bewildered.

The house was empty and gave evidence of recently departed tenants. A broken umbrella, some old overshoes, and a few boxes were scattered about. Fred noticed that there was a small "For Sale" sign on the lawn. By now, Susan had seen the second floor and came dashing down the stairs into the living room. She was blazing with excitement. She told them of her Christmas wish to Mr. Kringle, and here it had come true! Each room was exactly as she had known it would be from the plan in the magazine.

"Mother, you were right about believing even though common sense tells you not to! See, I kept on believing and you were right!" she said breathlessly, and with that she was off to the back yard to see if her swing was there.

Fred looked at Doris. "Did you really tell Susan that?" he asked. Doris nodded silently, on the verge of tears. And then they were in each other's arms.

"Well, everybody believes in Mr. Kringle now," Fred said happily. "It seems to be unanimous!"

Doris nodded, still unable to speak. "This house made Susan believe in him," said Fred, "and it seems to be for sale. We can't let Kris down now, can we?"

Doris shook her head, smiling, and then she finally found her voice. "I never really doubted you in my heart," she said. "It was just my silly common sense."

"Well—it even makes sense to believe in me now,"

said Fred. "After all, I must be a pretty good lawyer. I took a little old man from an old folks' home and legally proved to the world that he was Santa Claus!"

Doris nodded, smiling. "You're wonderful!" she said. Then something caught Fred's eye.

Standing in the corner near the fireplace was a cane, a common, ordinary cane just like the one Mr. Kringle always carried. Doris saw it, too.

"Oh, no!" she said. "It couldn't be. It must have been left by the people who moved out—"

"Well, maybe," said Fred. He scratched his head and gave a wry smile. "But on the other hand, maybe I didn't do anything so wonderful after all!"

Historical Note

"AS a child I had very definite doubts about Santa Claus. It always puzzled me that while my Christmas gifts were supposed to come from Santa, I must be sure to thank Uncle George or Aunt Mabel for each one. I was very sceptical [sic] indeed. But recent events have changed my mind completely—I'm a firm believer now. . . ."

So begins an article that screenwriter Valentine Davies wrote in the summer of 1947 for *Book News,* supporting the publication of his first book, *Miracle on 34th Street.* He describes how, while serving as a Coast Guard officer in 1944, he had been disappointed by the commercial focus and lack of true spirit during the annual rush before Christmas. He thought that if there really were a Santa Claus, and if that Santa walked into a modern department store, he'd be "a pretty disillusioned old boy." Val, as his friends knew him, outlined a story about Kris Kringle, an elderly gentleman in a retirement home who filled in as Santa Claus in the Macy's Thanksgiving Day Parade. Kringle seemed so authentic that Macy's hired him as its Santa Claus, and within days, seemingly without effort, old Kris Kringle elicited goodwill among merchants throughout New York

City—and inspired a skeptical little girl, and her equally doubtful mother, to believe in him, too.

Davies showed the outline for what he had intended to be a screenplay to his toughest critic—his wife, Liz, who, to his surprise, was enthusiastic. With her encouragement, he fleshed out the idea and sent the story to George Seaton, a writer-director at Twentieth Century-Fox and an old friend from their University of Michigan days. Seaton shared the idea with executives at the studio, and soon after, they offered Davies a contract for his story. With Seaton on board to write the screenplay, Twentieth Century-Fox went into production for the film starring Edmund Gwenn, Maureen O'Hara, John Payne, and newcomer Natalie Wood.

During the filming, another college crony, Dr. Walter Simpson (Michigan class of 1924), forwarded Davies' story to S. Spencer Scott (class of 1914), vice president and general manager of Harcourt, Brace and Company. The manuscript reached both Scott and editor-in-chief Robert Giroux (later of the publishing house Farrar, Straus and Giroux), who both quickly moved to publish the book in tandem with the scheduled fall 1947 release of the film.

Because of a film industry strike, there was a shortage of color films available from all of the studios for screening that summer, so Twentieth Century-Fox decided to release *Miracle on 34th Street* twice—once, in June, to select theaters to fill the gap in new movies; then in early fall nationwide. Archival letters detail how Harcourt, Brace in general—and Robert Giroux and his staff in particular—pushed to advance the book's release date to tie in with that of the film. Giroux, who had received the rough manuscript in February, worked with Davies to reshape the book, using the original and revised versions of the manuscript. Davies put the final touches on the rewrite and offered feedback on the jacket art, leaving Harcourt, Brace to perform its own miracle by racing the manuscript through layout, typesetting, and production in just three months to guarantee finished books in June, in time for the film's premiere.

Within months of its release, the book was appearing on bestseller lists, with more than four hundred thousand copies in print. The film went on to win three Academy Awards: Best Supporting Actor, for Edmund Gwenn's portrayal of Kris Kringle; Best Screenplay, for George Seaton; and Best Original Story, for that disillusioned Coast Guard officer, Valentine Davies. Clearly, postwar America was ready for some old-fashioned Christmas spirit, packaged in this modern tale.

The story has withstood the test of time. More than fifty years after the publication of *Miracle on 34th Street*, Macy's still hosts its annual Thanksgiving Day

Parade and the U.S. Postal Service continues to receive thousands of letters to Santa Claus each holiday season. In Kris Kringle's words: "Underneath all the hurry and bustle people still believe in Santa Claus and all Christmas stands for." Valentine Davies had become a "firm believer" while in the process of creating what he considered his best work. As Robert Giroux wrote to Davies after first reading the story: "We editors simply think that this is the best Christmas story since Charles Dickens' *A Christmas Carol.*" Families nationwide echo his opinion by gathering each holiday season to watch the film, reaffirming their faith in miracles and the power of goodwill.

Friends, relatives, and colleagues recall Davies as an energetic, talented, humorous man who loved sailing, jazz, and Michigan football. But he was first and foremost a writer, developing his craft at college with a column in the *Michigan Daily* and honing his skills as a graduate student at the Yale Drama School. He walked away from his family's lucrative real estate business in New York and moved to Hollywood (which he called a suburb of New York) to try his hand at screenwriting. He wrote for MGM, RKO, and Universal Studios, as well as for Twentieth Century-Fox. He penned one other novel, *It Happens Every Spring,* and a Broadway musical, *Blow Ye the Winds.* In addition to receiving an Oscar in 1947 for *Miracle,* he was subsequently nominated three times for the golden statue: Best Motion Picture Story, for *It Happens Every Spring* (1949); Best Story and Screenplay, for *The Glenn Miller Story* (1954); and Best Short Subjects Documentary, for *The House Without a Name* (1956), which he produced. He was a member of the Writers Guild of America, which since 1962 has presented the prestigious Valentine Davies Award to the WGA member "whose contributions to the entertainment industry and the community-at-large [bring] dignity and honor to writers everywhere."

Valentine Davies was president of the Academy of Motion Picture Arts and Sciences when he died in 1961 at his home in Malibu, California. He was fifty-five years old. Marian Saphro, who was Davies' secretary at the time of his death, recalled many years later that her boss passed away in the midst of a hearty laugh. Somehow, it seems only fitting for the man who gave the world Kris Kringle, with all his joy and magic.